THE FALLEN LEAVES

About the Author

Saibal Gupta (born in 1937) is a doctor of medicine. In addition to his studies in medicine, he has had lifelong attachment to the study of history, philosophy, physical sciences, biological sciences and human culture in general. In his later years, he started writing on these subjects in an interactive manner showing basic unity of human thought and culture, analysing both the past and the present on the background of unity of human intellect and human psychology. He has published a book and several articles in Bengali in different journals. He then switched over to English and published many articles in journals of repute. This is his first novel in English.

THE FALLEN LEAVES

A Love Story

Saibal Gupta

CONCEPT PUBLISHING COMPANY, NEW DELHI-110059

Cataloging in Publication Data—DK
Courtesy: D.K. Agencies (P) Ltd. <docinfo@dkagencies.com>

Gupta, Saibal, 1937-
The fallen leaves : a love story / Saibal Gupta.
p. cm.
A novel.
ISBN 8180691861

1. Indic fiction (English). I. Title.

DDC 823 21

"All characters and events in this book are fictitious and any similarity with any individual, living or dead, or any past event is purely coincidental."

ISBN-81-8069-186-1

First Published 2005

Published and Printed by
Ashok Kumar Mittal
Concept Publishing Company,
A/15-16, Commercial Block, Mohan Garden,
New Delhi-110059 (INDIA)

Phones : 25351460, 25351794
Fax : 091-11-25357103
Email : publishing@conceptpub.com

Contents

The Prologue

THIRTY years before the turn of the century I was struggling to find a career in a society that was backward and competitive at the same time. The rules were primitive. One had to crawl rather than stand on one's own right. Accomplishments stood a very low second to whom you knew and what you did to please them. After struggling for years I was just about able to survive. I had been able to rent a small flat for my family. I desperately needed a telephone at my house, never having had one before. It was extremely difficult to get a telephone in those days. One had to wait for years and know the right people. As a young man returning from abroad and starting out on a career I knew nobody. By chance I met somebody at a friend's house who suggested a way out. If I could procure the right recommendations I could apply for a temporary connection for six months. If I got one I could apply again for an extension of another six months. Like this I can go on for two years and if I was lucky, I may be able to get it converted to a permanent connection by that time.

He provided the necessary recommendation and I applied for a temporary connection. Armed with the papers I walked into the central telephone office and presented them to the public relations officer. It was a medium size hall with a number of small tables. One person was sitting behind each table. But none of them was doing anything.

They just sat behind empty tables with a vacant look on their faces. One or two were gossiping. The only busy person was the public relations officer himself with a number of supplicants standing around. When my turn came I introduced myself and stated the purpose of my visit. As he took the papers from my hand, a slight movement nearby made me turn my gaze sideways. I found that a man sitting behind one of the tables in the second row on my right was standing up with folded hands. When our eyes met he said respectfully 'Oh, so you are the famous writer'. He was standing there with a face as if looking at a minor god. I did not know what to say. There was no writer in any language with a name even remotely similar to mine. I was pretty sure of that. But I was desperate for a telephone and I did not mind to be identified as anything worthwhile if I could get the connection. So I remained silent.

I got the temporary connection and six months passed in the bliss of having a phone in the house. It passed all too quickly and the time came for a renewal. Again armed with necessary papers I marched to the PRO's office and waited around his table. I watched with the corner of my eye and found that the same man who complimented me as a writer was sitting behind the same table with a vacant face and was doing nothing, just like everybody else in the room. Again I introduced myself and mentioned my name in a hushed voice so as not to be overheard by that man. I thought he must have realised his mistake by now and will call me an imposter. As I pronounced my name I glanced sideways and to my amazement he was again rising from his seat deferentially with folded hands and as our eyes met, said respectfully 'Oh, so you are the famous writer'. He maintained his standing position without uttering another word as long as I was there. Handing over my papers I walked out, too uneasy to look back at him. It was unnatural, if one knows the Bengali character, that he did not try to start a conversation on any of the books that I am supposed to have written, but just stood there in silent admiration. As a matter of fact I had never written anything in my life not to speak of publishing. Writing was as far from me as an Eskimo from Africa.

Another six months passed and the time came for another renewal. By now I was dreading another journey to the PRO's office. Armed with my papers I made a beeline for his table in the now familiar office charting a diagonal course through the hall so that my back will be turned to those frightening tables. I submitted the papers in a hushed voice and they were received as usual after some small talk in which my name might have been mentioned. As I was leaving, curiosity made me glance backwards, and behold, that same man was beginning to rise from his chair in the same deferential pose with folded hands. Before he could utter his familiar line 'Oh, so you are the famous writer', I shot out of the hall into the foyer and was gone.

I never had to go back to that office as I got a permanent connection before the expiry of this term. I do not know whether the gentleman is still there or whether he was ever there. One thing is sure that none of his colleagues sitting at other tables ever showed any interest in what he was telling me though they were not busy doing anything. This again was unusual since every middle class Bengali worth his name is extremely interested in writers, particularly if one such presents himself in flesh and blood. That interest was even greater in pre-television days.

Well into my sixties now I have started to write and the reason is Amol. Age does not matter since everyday is a new day in life that Amol has taught me. He has taught me much more and has disturbed my well-set ideas so much that I have started to write them down on paper. This story is the story of Amol. But when I think of that man in telephone office I sometimes wonder whether he was really there or was he an oracle that some day I shall meet Amol again and what I hear will make me write.

I came across Amol after a gap of more than three decades. I knew him as a young man, a kid just out of college and came to know and like him. Actually we became very intimate within a short time. To me he seemed to be one of the very best products of the Indian society. He was intelligent, erudite with a love for books, athlete of some distinction, a good student and along with that, probably because of his Hindu upbringing, he had a sort of detachment and self-effacement that made him endearing. He was not aggressive but nor was he prepared to budge if he thought he was right, with a doggedness that was sometimes surprising. He will never show off but knew how to get noticed. His was a very reserved nature not given to exuberance natural to his age but at the same time he had a sort of dry humour that will make people burst out laughing. He was an excellent companion who could talk on a wide range of subjects without appearing to show off. When we would discuss girls as was natural at that age he would join in and make everybody laugh but his words would never cross the limits of decency. Somehow one felt a depth in him. Once I remember telling him jokingly that he would make a very good monk. To my surprise he became serious and remarked that it will not be a bad alternative and has a lot of merit to be considered.

He left India rather suddenly sometime after his college days. That is the last I saw him until we met by chance after a gap of three decades and more. Our past fondness caught up with us and he promised to spend one evening with me. He was very successful in the worldly way. But more interesting was how he looked at his experiences in life and himself and the way he described them half-humorously. It was as if he was observing himself from outside through a journey and trying to understand what it was all about. It was difficult to string along his stories chronologically and connect them with irrelevant fillers to make them into a continuous story of a man, without losing the relevance of the moments, as Amol himself told me. It is in those moments that we really live. So I decided to write his stories as he told me on that memorable evening of early spring and cut out the small talks.

Autumn Symphony

AMOL was pacing up and down the large courtyard in front of the main church of the small university town. The dry leaves of autumn on the paved courtyard were rustling around in the restless wind. He was waiting for Britt. They had met a year back and had an instant liking for each other. They were the same age in their mid-twenties. Britt was a beauty—not of the golden blond type, but of brown hair blue eyed variety with the body of a goddess. Amol was a young man fresh from India, brown skinned with the liberal education, refinements and inhibitions of a conservative upbringing. The attraction was immediate as the attraction of opposites. Britt was vibrant, wild and aggressive with a tremendous *joie de vivre*. Amol was a recluse, very erudite, quiet and thoughtful. Together they made a pretty picture to those who knew them—two healthy young beauties coming from two completely different cultures. Britt being the aggressive one was the first to break the ice and build up a friendship. Amol on his side had never seen a girl like this and with an apprehension befitting the men in the age group of twenties in those days was cautious and circumspect. Britt found this exasperating.

Their friendship grew naturally through work, through long walks, through social evenings. Standing in the church courtyard and looking at the cobbled road that ran by its side with its quaint little shops Amol could almost see the sprawling lawns of the university only a few blocks away. It was a long summer last year and autumn was late in coming. The lawns were bright green but the trees were beginning to turn purple and were bathed in the golden sunlight of the autumn afternoon. They were cycling down the narrow paths joking and fooling and fell down on the green grass of the lawn. She was wearing a red skirt with a white blouse and an open topcoat. She took off the scarf holding her hair and shook them. The golden light tangled in her hair and she laughed. A fountain of iridescent glow seemed to cascade down. Amol was staring at the sight. Britt kept on laughing and asked what was the matter. Amol said in a hoarse whisper 'You are so beautiful!' This was the early days. Both, to their own amazements, were finding out how alike they were in spite of their widely different backgrounds. The more they discovered each other the more the fondness grew. They would drive around in Amols ramshackle old car among the red and gold of the autumn woods, have coffee under a birch or pine in secluded spots in the woods. They would take long walks through the jungle. Silence of the jungle, the dripping trees and the moss covered wooden bench creating an intimacy without words. They will drive to a hot dog stand and fight as to who should pay. They would come home to Britt's place happily exhausted. Amol had never had a drink in his life apart from an occasional sip of beer from a friend's glass. Britt would tease him that the best thing was to start with champagne and give him the strong vodka instead and Amol would choke on the drink. Autumn rolled into winter. They would drive through the sleet on the frozen roads of winter. Sometimes they would race each other, Britt in her vespa daring Amol to drive on the snow. Amol became quite adept at driving in the snow. They would go for ice-skating on the frozen lakes and Britt would teach him. Amol slips and they come down on top of each other, laughing all the time. Britt wouldn't leave him until Amol gets it right. Britt taught him how to light a fire in snow by collecting dry brambles, how to roast a chicken leg or a sausage and keep warm. Winter rolled into the spring and then the summer. They would sit beside the lakes, roll down the grassy slopes, and run along the beaches pushing each other into the icy waters. As the summer became warmer they would look out for small deserted beaches. Amol was an expert swimmer. They will put on snorkels and swim side by side. This was an expanse of life that Amol had never dreamt of. It all seemed like a fairytale to him. He would sometimes stand in front of a mirror for minutes to assure himself that whatever was happening was real and not in a dream. He had to look at his brown skin that was turning golden to remind him who he was. At the work place his brilliance had been noticed and the appreciation and opportunities were beyond his imagination. All the facets of his life were full to the brim and overflowing.

It took a long time for Amol to come out of his shell. In the restricted middle class life of India there are many prejudices and pressures that weigh down individuality. Amol was slowly finding the depth of his personality. What was he? Was he a product of only time and space or was there something fundamental and unchangeable in him, in anybody? So much joy, can it last through a lifetime? Is it necessary to think of such things? He thought about the ethical and moral principles on which he had grown up until now. Was there anything absolute in them at all? Morality breeds in narrow confines as also profligacy. Where wide world is the stage and man is not weighted down by the greed and narrowness of society, the natural morality of man takes over. What is the definition of that natural morality, on what does it hinge? They were out of any society. They were so engrossed with each other that they were not even conscious of its presence. The society was probably looking at them with indulgent affection. The pensive introvert that Amol was, he thought about their relationship more than Britt did. She only enjoyed and nothing was more enjoyable than to be with Amol.

In spite of all these she vanished sometimes and went out of reach. Amol missed her, would wonder where she might be and got upset and jealous. The little green serpent was making an occasional appearance. She would turn up, laugh away all his miseries and tease him 'I am neither your wife nor your mistress you know'. He would insist on knowing and she will laugh. 'Oh, you are so dumb. Don't you know that a woman must have her private moments, that it cannot be just love, love and love all the time'? 'Why not', he would ask. 'Because I am not a man that is why dumbo. What if my parents were here, huh, what would you have done then, break down the house?' Amol would continue to sulk. She would jump on him and tease 'and what about you? You are sometimes such a coward and don't know how to take and then you suddenly become lord and master, hey what about that.' Then they would go to a theatre, a dance club and all will be same as ever. Amol was learning very gradually the mystery that a woman is, that man has never fathomed since the days of Adam. This mystery has nothing to do with the values and customs of the society; this mystery is inherent in the youth. But he was not in a position to know it then. Nor did he know how precious this mystery was. Men never know until it passes them.

Physicality entered their relationship as naturally as spring follows winter. It was not a result of wooing or chasing or an attack of violent passion. The day it happened, they sort of flowed into it, Britt leading the way. Amol was nervous and hesitant. Britt was hilarious. They kissed and kissed and then they had a little fight. Then Britt teased

Amol to laughter. Then they had a dinner cooked by Britt and then they started kissing again. Then it naturally flowed into passion. Amol lost his virginity in an experience at once exhilarating and numbing, almost spiritual in its power. But it did not happen right away as Amol confided later; he did not make it the first time. Something from his past came and stood between. Britt was puzzled and tried whatever she could, which was not much. Then she gave up and said she could not help him in whatever that was wrong. They fell asleep in each other's arms. When he woke up Britt was still asleep. He looked at her face and a deep tenderness flowed in his heart. He looked and looked at this beautiful creature in his arms and his passion rose pushing aside whatever was holding him back. Britt stirred in his arms and woke up. They plunged into the ecstasy of their togetherness. Like a picture his whole life was passing before his eyes as he made love lustily. For better or for worse he felt he was being born again. As their love life grew Britt would often tease him. 'You are like a tiger now. What happened the first time? You seemed to have seen a ghost.' Their passions rose as if in unison like a duet. They fitted exactly into each other physically and emotionally. They made love in most unlikely places, in a deserted cottage in the woods, on a lonely beach with the blue sky and deep blue waters of the sea as witness. He would look into her blue eyes and the world would vanish and he would stare and stare in wonder.

Their fondness for each other grew. They started to go out in society and started to face what they had not faced before. They started discovering each other as they faced the frictions and reactions of the society. They were protective to each other. Their own personal reactions were probably different. Both of them realised that they have a different past and a future, which may or may not be different. In spite of their intimacy Britt remained an enigma to Amol. She would sometimes go into a mood and refuse to see him for days. Amol would again wonder whether she was seeing another man and would ask her. Britt's answer would be terse and tasty, yes, why not? One day she laid herself bare. She had a boyfriend and lover before meeting Amol. He was an English boy. She was madly in love with him. She even got pregnant and had to have an abortion, for his sake. He went away to some other country and promised to send for her. But the letter never came. She was totally heartbroken and went crazy. As she said all this, her eyes were red but she was not crying. Her face was set in a sad and grim way. 'I do not want to go through it again' was all she said. This was something Amol had never faced and did not know how to handle. Falling in love meant marriage in India, more so in those days. Falling in love itself was difficult. On the other hand humanity did not injure itself as much or may be they did, but in some other way. Through his reasoning and self-examination he found nothing wrong in Britt's past life and grew even fonder of her. But this was against his upbringing and culture. Who knows whether his heart accepted what his head decided? Did he know himself?

A few days later they were together in Amol's house. He caressed and hugged her. They talked for some time and went to bed. As they lay there caressing each other Amol felt a deep love. He started talking about what he thought life was all about. He talked about the innate divinity of man and so long as one remained honest to one's own self nothing is sullied inside and so on and so forth. He quoted from the philosophies of the east and the west, he jumped out of the bed to bring down books and read passages from them. Amol's natural spiritual bent of mind was heightened by the intense love he was feeling. First love heightens man's spiritual awareness and Amol's natural bent of mind and intellectualism made it more intense. Britt lay wide-awake listening to Amol, kissing him now and then. Both of them were so engrossed that they became aware only when the first lights of dawn filtered in through the curtains. It was time to get ready and go to work. It was a night that never happened before or after. As they got out of bed Amol said apologetically 'I have spoilt our night together. I hope you are not upset or angry'. Britt took his face in her hands and said 'It is really a strange experience. I have never known that a man and woman can lie naked in bed the whole night and never make love. But I shall honestly tell you that I did not understand all of what you said but I feel perfectly happy and strangely fulfilled'.

Their tenderness took a new turn. There was more seriousness along with the usual frolicking. One day as they were sitting on a lonely stretch of grassland beside a pool with Amol's arms around Britt, she calmly looked up into his eyes and said 'you should have had a clean girl'. Amol was shocked into silence. What did she mean by saying that he should have a clean girl? How does a human being become clean or unclean? If he can come out of his centuries old prejudices of a restricted society inhuman to women, then why this free and beautiful creature of a supposedly free society have such an opinion of herself that she cannot give him enough? Or is it something else? This cannot be because she is afraid of commitment or because she was in love with someone else because she would have told him without hesitation. Does this prejudice run so deep that it is deeper than culture? He hugged her even more tightly.

Amol continued to pace the courtyard of the church waiting for Britt.

We were silent, sitting together in the gathering darkness of dusk. After some time I asked 'What happened after that?' Amol turned to me with a slight irritation. "Nothing happened. Must the story go on? What happened was an autumn symphony that plays in my mind whenever I sit with myself." After a decent interval I asked softly 'Where is Britt?' He was silent for some time. Then he said 'Last time I heard she was living in a forest area all by herself on the Baltic coast high up in the north, living raw in nature.'

Fleeting Passion

ANITA was a girl from north of England. She was a typical tall English girl with a straight somewhat upturned nose, like Julie Andrews. The similarity ended there. She was a simple pretty girl. They had seen each other at parties before they came to talk and know each other. They danced together through one evening and their rhythm was right. At the end of the evening he kissed her and she kissed back with passion. They met at a few more parties and one day he proposed her to go out and have a date. She asked him to come to her small flat, where she lived alone, and have dinner. A date was fixed. As the evening came Amol grew restless. He did not know whether he should go through with it. Did he really like her or know her well enough? A party time was a different thing. He began dressing unmindfully and took a long time. Then he sat down with a drink and thought some more. At last he thought it would be unkind to make the girl wait and stand her up. After all it was his suggestion and as a gentleman he should keep his word. He would see how things turned out and then think. Maybe he will like the girl after all. As a result of all this he was late when he arrived at her door and rang the bell. There was no response. He waited for some time and rang the bell again. Still there was no response. He thought that maybe she was in the bath or doing something that the girls did and got late in getting ready.

He waited for a few more minutes strolling around the courtyard and the footpath outside and rang the bell. There was no response. He rang the bell once again and waited. Still there was no response. He decided that either he had been stood up or something else had happened. This was a bit of a puzzle but not entirely unmixed with relief. Still it hurt the male vanity.

He did not meet her for quite some time after that evening and did not look for her. A few months passed and at a party he noticed her again from a distance. He expected her to come forward with an apology or an explanation. But she did not, simply looked him over once and that was all. She had come with a young man as escort. In the middle of the party there was suddenly a time when they were close and alone. There was a moment of uneasiness. Then Amol got better of his vanity and asked her why she stood him up that evening. She was amazed, 'I stood you up? You deserted me. You never showed up.' Amol protested. He had waited nearly fifteen minutes outside her house. Her eyes dilated. 'You did? Oh that must have been when I went to the phone booth to call you. You were late.' Now it was Amol's turn to be surprised. 'What do you mean you went to a phone booth'? Anita laughed 'Sorry I forgot to tell you that I had no phone in my house. It is such a bother. So when you were not turning up I walked to the phone booth. It is only round the corner. But the girl who was already in the booth just kept on talking. At last I got the phone but there was no response from your side. So I hurried back home but you never came.' Then they both burst out laughing so much that tears came to their eyes. Others came around and asked what was so funny. Anita gasped 'Nothing really'. There were no regrets on either side.

As Amol was relating this story he also theorised, as

was his habit. 'You see, most of our passions are fleeting. Only a few are important enough to last. A professional who is in love with passion grabs the moment and thinks afterwards, for better or for worse. But I am a cautious amateur, have always been one. I like it this way.'

Prejudices

IT was a bit surprising to hear Amol speak so much about party and dancing. For all the years I knew him I have never known him dancing. Dancing was not the thing young people in those days did in the society he grew up. He was also a bit of a conservative prude among us. I could not help but remark casually in the middle of the conversation, not wanting to upset him, 'So you did learn to dance?' He laughed out 'Yeah, I taught myself and did really well at that. How it started is a funny story.'

Amol was living for some time in a small seaside town in Wales. It was a small town in those days with very few people, when it was not a tourist season. Everybody knew everybody and they very much kept to themselves even when the tourists were there. They were a simple decent country people who were very friendly by nature. The big social event of the town was the Mayor's Ball held each year sometime around Christmas when the tourists were not there. Every resident of the town was invited to the Ball, young and old. The Ball was held in the town hall that had a big dance hall with polished wooden floor and balconies all around. Amol had seen such halls in old clubs in India from British times. As a temporary resident of the town he was invited with a gilt edged card. He arrived in proper formal attire as he was told.

At one end of the hall was a dais on which sat the Mayor with his wife and a few other distinguished citizens. The band was in front of the dais and was playing old tunes from Welsh folk music and mixing them with the modern and the classical now and then. The music was very good. The ladies were conservatively dressed and so were the men, young and old. There was plenty of beer but no drunkenness and a lot of gaiety all around. The atmosphere was so nice that it reminded Amol of what he had read only in books. Couples were joining on the floor to dance, men proposing to women formally. The rowdiness of the English youth in the large cities was nowhere in sight. Amol's feet were itching to dance. The music was so rhythmic and pulsating; the girls were so nice and sober looking. But he knew only a few people and many of them were steady couples. On top of that he did not know dancing, not the formal ballroom dancing. It was daunting to go out on the floor in full view of the dais, the balconies, men and women standing all around and clapping. At last courage took over, courage egged on by the maddening rhythm. With a palpitating heart he approached a girl who was vaguely familiar, a secretary in the place he worked, and who seemed to have come alone. They went on the floor when the band was playing a slow number. He had to hold her. He held her as he had seen in pictures and cautiously kept as much distance as possible so as not to appear to be a 'lech'. The girl was very lovely; he had to admit that. After a few steps the girl said 'Let me ask you a question, have you ever danced before?' Amol's answer was honest 'Never'. The girl whispered 'You are a very brave man but just as a first lesson let me show you how you hold my hand.' All through the night Amol kept on dancing with that girl and with others as they mobbed him. In one night he went through it all from modern to folk to ballroom dancing in gay abandon shedding all his shy self-consciousness. It was the party of his life. He discovered that his body naturally gyrated with rhythm, as the most primitive man must have found out. In India he had seen people gyrate with devotion to spiritual music and he loathed it. He had seen tribal men and women dance with beat music and though the rhythm was pleasing it was not for him. Prejudice had kept him away from this gay abandon of life, which was one of the natural life forces of man. Next day when he went to the small market of the town, he was surrounded by a small group of local girls. They asked him seriously whether he had found a belt that one of the girls had lost last night. He looked dumb. 'A belt? Me?' The girls burst out laughing and left him speechless as he realised the implication and the joke too late. The friendliness warmed his heart and remains a treasured memory.

Amol also told me that Europe in the swinging sixties was suffering from acute male deficiency syndrome. The youth, specially the men, had been decimated during the war. In the post war generation, the girls had attained maturity but the boys were still boys. Living and travelling extensively through those times he realised that morality, especially the sexual morality had no absolute value. It was dependent on the geography and the social situation. Tagging such morality to religion and God was the folly of man. Students and workers poured in Europe from other parts of the world and European societies became heterogeneous. Those who went back to their own countries carried memories both sweet and bitter and these have affected their own societies. Particularly striking has been the effect of ideas of democracy and liberalism carried back to purely tribal societies and has given rise to conflicts and instability. Seeding of such ideas in the minds of the foreign youth was often through the fondness for girls they met or the bitterness of rejected loves. Rejected loves may have caused revolutions elsewhere. A cataloguing of such loves in the lives of leaders of Asia and Africa and the effects thereof will be an interesting historical study but the data, he thought, will be difficult to get.

'So you did get rid of your prejudice after all' said I. He said 'Yes, eventually. But one does not get rid of all one's prejudices. We live with them. Maybe we modify them a little bit. Very few of us consciously try to get rid of our prejudices. Even then we fail. I can relate a story, an experience of which I am ashamed to this day and given a second chance I shall put it right. But second chances rarely come.'

Amol was in the southern part of the U.S.A at the height of the Vietnam War. The society was in turmoil. The youth were bewildered. Their value sense and beliefs had taken a severe beating. Thousands had died and thousands more were out there leaving their families, fiancées and girl friends. They included blacks and whites and their folks back home were suffering equally bad. Never before had the society been cemented together so much through common suffering. Amol's heart went out to them but at the same time he could not accept their paranoia and shortsightedness about supposedly hostile Asiatics, who were only trying hard to find an identity beyond a long and painful colonial past. He was vocal about it and so his views were known both to the doves and the hawks at the work place for which he was both liked and disliked. But his individuality was respected although there were a number of veterans around who had seen action. A large section of American youth still believed their politicians blindly. That was depressing in a mature democracy. To many it was a question of honour and solidarity with the suffering brethren and it went right through the colour prejudice that was so strong in the south. There was too much suffering all around.

Amol was invited to a small house party one day thrown by a white couple and the guests included a number of single black girls. The guests were introduced to each other. Amol was sitting next to a young black girl named Samantha. The host introduced them and told him with a wink 'Take care of her. She is going through a bad patch. A little upswing in love life will do her a lot of good.' They both laughed at the remark and started talking. Amol was himself going through a bad patch. The girl was nice and educated. They talked a lot about music and literature and so on, leaving aside delicate issues. They danced a little and liked each other. The evening ended. They exchanged phone numbers and promised to call. Amol said he had no car and the girl said she did not have either but that was no problem.

Amol never called. Many times he would decide to call and then hesitate. He reasoned and reasoned but could not decide. As he told me 'I realised much later that I was only kidding myself. The reason I did not call her was because she was black, though I was only a shade lighter than she was.' I protested 'It could not have been entirely that. The segregation was still largely there in the southern states. That social atmosphere must have affected you; what would the friends say if you went around with a black girl.' He said 'It can only be partly true. I think I did have the suspicion that colour was a factor in choosing the guest list of the evening. That was one sort of classical American stupidity. They are used to thinking that they are cleverer than others. But yet the honesty and simplicity is sometimes touching as in this time. But that does not take away from the fact that this thing about colour is in our blood. It comes from our caste system, the *varnashram*. Remember that *varna* also means colour. Have you ever seen an Indian boy and a Negro girl marrying or going together or *vice versa*? Very rarely, that is, if ever. It has put us to grief in many parts of the world. I could not forgive myself. I boast about not having any prejudices in life and still this was so deep rooted that I could not overcome it. You see it did not matter to the girl. She must have found another friend. But it matters to me. That is why I talked about a 'second chance.' I stared at him. His agony was obvious. It seemed as if he had done a crime against humanity. So I said 'Well the prejudice is much less today, it is on the way out.' Amol said 'I hope so.'

Talking about prejudices Amol talked about an Indian couple he had known in the States. Akash was a Maharashtrian Brahmin and Neelam was a Muslim. They had met as students in Bombay and fell in love. Akash's orthodox family could not accept a Muslim girl as the daughter-in-law. They got married nevertheless and faced hostilities from both sides, as the orthodox Muslim family of Neelam did not accept a son-in-law who did not convert to Islam. On top of the financial hardship that a young couple faces, this social ostracism made life impossible. Akash got a job in the States and the family moved. They had a daughter about two years old when Amol met them. It was a very happy family and he spent many a nice evening with them. They were very much in love. They led a secular life not practicing any religion overtly. What they felt inside about their own religions was difficult to make out. Amol left that place after some time but kept in touch. Then the touch was lost. He came back after couple of years and tried to look them up. He learnt that they had separated and gone their respective ways, nobody knew where. The prejudice outside and a common front had made their bond. But when that hostile environment was no longer there, their bond had lost its strength. In many a love and marriage even the partners are sometimes not aware how much of it is real and how much circumstantial. He also realised that prejudice works both ways. It destroys bonds and it also makes bonds. That is probably how society works. Can we ever be really free? Many societies live happily within a firm bondage of prejudices and until modern times the qualifying word would have been all, or most. All sorts of funny prejudices are there, of food, of clothing, of attitude to women, not to speak of really big ones. Religions consolidate by forming bondage of brotherhood through carefully built up prejudices. Quite often the original premise is lost in the process. Humanity is being compelled to give up prejudices as they evolve into a world community and that is giving rise to a lot of tensions. But can man really give up prejudices? Can a man survive without putting up a wall around him, a reference wall of prejudices that gives his life a quality? Amol did not know. As he said 'we should be allowed a simple set of prejudices, like mine for coffee, yours for tea. But who knows that they too will not be blown out of proportion some day?'

Brazilian Interlude

AMOL had known a boy from Brazil while he was in the U.S.A. and they became good friends. He was in his late twenties and was working in the States for a short time. His name was Vigo. He spoke broken English but was not very good at it. He had left his fiancée back in his hometown. The international trunk dialling was not available those days. The poor chap had a difficult time with the operator every time he wanted to call his fiancée. He would take Amol's help to make the connection. A few months later he grew very restless. As he told Amol, he was without a woman for so long that he was going crazy. Amol sympathised with him and thought how badly he must be missing his lover. He asked how long they had been seeing each other. Vigo was puzzled 'you mean her! Oh no, I do not have sex with my fiancée. I am going to marry her. We cannot have sex before marriage.'

Now it was Amol's turn to be surprised, 'what do you mean you do not have sex with her? Are you a virgin and still missing sex so badly?' 'I am not a virgin' he replied. 'Then what do you do? Do you go to prostitutes?' 'No.' Then Vigo explained, 'you see there are girls, single girls in our society who are independent and go out with men. You meet them, go out with them and have sex now and then, if they allow and they do allow.' Amol was thoroughly puzzled. 'You mean there are three kinds of women in your society? One class who do it for money, one who are kept pristine pure for marriage and a third who do it just for sex? This is unbelievable.' Vigo insisted 'Yes it is true.' 'These independent women you are talking about must earn their living and therefore have some education and a personality. Do you mean to say they do not fall in love, real love, with some man and no man ever falls in love with them?' Vigo said 'Yes that happens but nobody marries them.' Amol ridiculed 'How do you know them? Do they go around with some kind of a badge?' Vigo insisted 'everybody knows them. But sometimes mistakes do happen. One of my friends fell in love with one such girl and got engaged. Then he found out and he had to be bailed out.' Amol asked 'How?' 'Oh, I had to go and give evidence that I had been to bed with her.' 'Was it truth? Did you actually?' Vigo replied with conviction 'No. But I had to save a friend. He was my friend.' Amol gaped 'You did not think of the girl'? 'But he was my friend' protested Vigo. It was the ultimate Latin rationality. Amol was speechless. His heart went out to that unknown girl. What a male dominated society, even worse than ours, he thought.

A few days later Amol found Vigo walking very lovey-dovey with a girl. She was obviously an American, not from Brazil. Their paths crossed. Amol said 'Hello' and walked by. He had no inclination to wait and chat. Later when they met Vigo was furious. 'Why did you not wait and talk to us and say something to her. You insulted her.' Amol asked 'should I have? I do not know her. Who is she anyway?' 'I met her at a friend's place a few days back. She liked me and we had sex couple of days later. Next day we were walking down and you never even said hello to her. What a friend you are.' Amol said 'I am sorry. But did you like her?' With an expressive movement of his hands Vigo said 'Like her? Oh, I had no time to think; I had been in bed with a woman after six months. I had no time to decide whether I liked her or not.' 'So, you will be seeing her a lot now' asked Amol. 'Oh no, she is going away to Frisco in a couple of days. They are moving house. Her husband has gone ahead a week back to fix things and she is following him.' Amol tried to remember the girl. She looked very sweet and calm like any other middle class American wife. He thought the girl must have rationalised that having a little bit of sex on the side hurts nobody if nobody knew. But is that true? Apart from questions of morality does it not affect people's psychology to be so cynical? He would not know until he got married. But he would not certainly like his wife to sleep around and nor would she. But these things go on in every society and people live an outwardly perfect life through adjustment. But which one is better the old conservatism or the new liberalism? One thing is certain that this sexuality comes from unfulfilled or heightened desire. The tensions of modern civilisation and its consumerism are producing more unfulfilled desires than before and one of the outlets is sex. Is that good or bad? The other thing it produces is violence. And that is bad. Can you have one without the other?

Amol had opportunity to go to Brazil only many years later, probably two decades. He was aghast at such a blatantly double standard society but did not believe Vigo entirely. No society can exist like that. Therefore his curiosity was high. What he found gladdened his heart. Such a friendly and open society with an integrated population, more integrated than in many he knew, sharing the same culture, was nice to see. They were a joyous lot, enjoying life as much as it can give. There were problems and there were darker sides but who does not have them. What amused him most was that the women Vigo described were on a warpath turning society upside down. They were marrying and marrying with a vengeance the older men of Vigo's generation and tearing up their families and their fortunes with their own game, the sex game. Amol met a couple of such girls and found them very open, amusing and friendly. It was difficult not to love them even at his age. Some of them were cultured, educated and very pretty. But he also noticed that the social fallout of this sexuality was enormous. Not only was it producing broken marriages and parentless children, but also breeding despair and corruption in a large scale—the goodies in life were expensive. A new marriage, a new mistress were expensive propositions. The people were very gifted and the natural resources were plenty. A very gifted population, it seemed, was tied down by its own sensuality and not developing into their full potential. A large number of people were turning to spiritualism as a result, to control erotic desires which, taken to the extreme, damages something in the personality of most. But all things together he loved the people because there was no or very little hypocrisy in their society. The shadow of Vigo lifted.

I must have looked quizzical because while he seemed to condemn the sensuality he was also praising it as an absence of hypocrisy. Amol explained by telling a story. The beach attire of the Brazilian women is famous. Europe has caught on to them much later. They often go around in their swimsuit even when they are not actually on the beach. The dress, if it can be called that, has virtually nothing. The women in Brazil like to keep their buttocks bare and there is very little cover elsewhere. Many people associate these pictures of Brazilian beauties with the anonymous cities and pleasure places, like Rio, where tourists throng. Amol had once gone to a village by the seaside far from the big cities and found the same dress used by the young girls, their mothers and aunts. Whole families had gathered on the beach and on the promenade and shops around. The Brazilians cannot stay home on a holiday when the weather was nice, which was rather warm. There was nothing hush hush about the dress but it was certainly very erotic. He asked a middle-aged friend while chatting on the seaside whether he found it so and was he excited or just took it as a part of the scenery. He said 'excitement, oh, yes, very much. But be careful or you will get carried away and lose everything. Thank God, I have learnt to stand it. So many of my friends have lost everything to that temptation.' Amol sat on the sand looking at them, which, incidentally, they like, for what is the value of beauty if it is not shown and appreciated. But the man had said 'don't touch'. What an interesting world we live in. On one side are the countries in the Middle East where the women have to cover themselves from top to toe and on the other this display of flesh but it is all the same. Men are tempted everywhere and fall apart everywhere whether the women are covered or not. The sight of a bare ankle can send a man to raptures. So do the women. You have to be careful in Saudi Arabia and you have to be careful in Brazil. Societies crack and crumble. Men are taken to court or killed by the pelting of stones. Amol had met Iranian, Jordanian, Palestinian women in Europe. He had also seen them in their own countries. They are no different from these Brazilian women and sometimes even more aggressive. Women have a compulsive desire to bare themselves in every culture when it is safe to do so. They also have compulsive loyalties, with or without marriage. Societies, religions make so many formulas, but nothing works, or probably everything works in its own helter-skelter way. Why do we fight on these things, why do we make laws? Is it our greed, our acquisitive nature that fouls up everything? Probably the world would have been a much better place to live in with one-tenth of its present population. Amol's reverie was broken by a sweet voice by his side. The man had gone and a girl had come and sat by his side and was asking something. He did not understand Portuguese, or should he say Brazilian. There are minor differences. The girl understood and asked in English 'where are you from?' She was obviously less than half his age. But that was no problem; age was no bar to relationships in Brazil. The girl was very excited to know his identity. Her pupils dilated. They went on talking about a lot of things about football, because a Brazil-Argentina match was coming up, and then about music. They discussed about kaiperia, a popular and very strong drink that Amol liked very much. The girl started laughing and ran to get two glasses of kaiperia. They talked more, laughed and joked. The conversation became animated under the influence of kaiperia. The girl was flushed and excited. Suddenly she said she had to go. They got up. The girl hugged him tight and gave a full long kiss on the open mouth. There was in her eyes that something that men have craved to see through the ages, that they have given their empires for. Amol was a bit peeved being an obvious foreigner on an open beach in full view of the families. But nobody cared. There were one or two smiles. She was gone. A couple of days later Amol saw her one evening at a party. She was with her boyfriend or fiancé, but definitely not a husband. She came forward smilingly and shook his hand and that was that, no introductions, no explanations. Amol thought that if he had been resident things might have been different. She knew he was not. The protective instinct took over. But that did not prevent her from saying that she liked him.

After Amol finished we were silent for some time. I was digesting his story. Then I said 'It seems that you have a prejudice against sex, you know, sex by itself, as its own justification.' Amol said 'Oh, no. I have no prejudice about that. Sex, in the case of humans, happens as much in the head as in his sex organs. Have you ever wondered why man, of all animals, has no special season for sexual desire and mating? He alone has been given complete control over his desire. He has only got to think about it and he has the desire. This has come about in the course of evolution. In nature there is a direct relationship between sex and population. In other animals and early man the environment and laws of nature kept the balance. Then man controlled environment and disease and human population grew. Now man has succeeded in separating sex from procreation. The Malthusian ideal is here. He can have sex without procreation and procreation without sex. He has earned complete freedom and the responsibility for sex and to maintain his biological balance. But mentalisation, if I can use the term, or conceptualisation, if you prefer that, of sex has made it a very important part of his psyche. Sexual suppression does not exist in other animals, but applies to man because he is the controller. In a similar fashion he may eliminate sex from his mind without suppression if he is deeply engrossed in something else.'

'How much of sex occurs in the mind and how much in the body has probably never been measured, at least not to my knowledge. In any case it must vary from person to person and also probably from situation to situation. Once I knew an Englishman in his late sixties, who used to boast that in his entire life he had never 'missed' a single weekend and never twice with the same female. He had a lot of disease but it was before the days of AIDS and was not fatal. I believed him and therefore also believed in the other extreme that it is possible for a couple to be deeply in love and not feel the desire for sex. Most of us live our life somewhere between these two extremes. But what I do not like is the continuous commercial and media pressure to perform. The society often proclaims that if you do not love sex, that is the physical part of it, you must be a freak. What was once a cherished and treasured sharing between two human beings has been brought down to the level of performance, to the open market place and all in the name of the new god, commerce and money. In a large part of human affairs becoming is associated with thinking and this continuous social thought pressure has created visible and invisible freaks. I have met men of arts, really sensitive men who are actually concerned about their ability to perform physically or not. Sex is equated to creativity. It may be related to the bit in the head but intellect definitely does not reside in the penis. They probably imagine themselves to be in the days of French impressionists when a taboo had to be broken, today it is a matter of keeping up with the Jones's or missing the gift of their youth. On the other hand I have met sensitive young men in Europe and America who are scared of this culture to perform whenever they get acquainted with and like a girl. Going to bed seems to be the only way to say 'I love you' to many girls and this disillusionment affects them and make them freaks, sometimes impotent or may be homosexuals. Many of them need psychiatric help. A young man in this culture will always have to have a label of homosexuality or heterosexuality even if he is not so well defined in any other way. As if nobody can have the desire to live all by himself or have close friends of the same sex. It happens with girls too. I remember at a party noticing a nice looking girl and thought I would like to have a dance with her. My friends dissuaded me saying that she was a bit crazy. I asked what that meant. They would only shrug and say 'Well she is queer.' That only means that she is either oversexed or undersexed or too emotional. There are many cultures where that would not be considered a crime. I hope we do not ape this in our society.

I was not inclined to give up. 'Come, come, you surely do not approve of that Englishman of yours.' He laughed. 'Why should I approve or disapprove? He was probably doing it in the mind too, proving something to himself or to others. Otherwise how does he get so much energy?

You have no qualms about sex but can you do the same as him? It is a simple thing. Some of us like the quantity and some of us like the quality. Quality is the highest when it happens in the mind but commerce is demanding only the quantity. That is unnerving and bad for health. I do not think we are a 'Brave New World' yet but we are running close. A learned female friend had once told me in Paris that mankind will never become that and would veer around from that cynicism. That is probably happening but not happening consciously because there is no alternative value addition. There is only fear of AIDS.'

We were silent, sitting in the small garden in our short balmy winter, sipping wine. Amol had brought a few bottles of a very good wine. He was a connoisseur of wines but how he managed to bring them through customs I would never know. He had a gift for those things without resorting to illegal or unfair means. He had a gift for handling men. He liked to live well and had a good taste for most of the things. Very much a man of the world but obviously he really lived very deep down. He was sipping his wine very slowly. Here too he liked quality to quantity. As he once told me that life was a delicate wine—sip it slowly and you will get the taste, but gulp it down and you will never know what went down. My reverie was broken by his short laughter. 'This is all getting a bit too serious', he said, 'let me tell you about two of my female conquests to liven things up a bit.'

The Girl in Beijing

AMOL was in Beijing soon after the doors were opened in communist China. He had some work to do. When that was finished he was offered a conducted tour through some other parts of the country, which he declined. He said he preferred to stay for a few more days in Beijing all by himself without any chaperoning. A few eyebrows must have been raised but the Chinese do not raise their eyebrows in public, as Amol told me. In any case he was a valued person and not to be upset. So he was left alone. He loved to move around alone wherever he went and communicate with people. Language was never a problem with him he told me. If people wished to communicate they could always do so and you can always find such people if they were not intimidated.

While coming in at the airport he had the usual experience in a communist or under-developed country. He was offered higher value for changing dollars unofficially. He was offered a private taxi in preference for the taxis at the stand. Attempts were made to misguide him from the taxi stand. All these things he expected and therefore avoided easily. In fact he deliberately went through the experience just to check. The official car was waiting for him. He noted that the unofficial value of dollar was only slightly higher than the official rate. So he knew that the macro-economy was in fairly good shape. As he drove down the wide four-lane highway he noticed the extreme paucity of cars. Those that were there were of large size and must be guzzling petrol. Therefore there must be very few, if at all, privately owned cars. From the air he had seen large highways leading out of the city but absolutely no cars for miles and miles. There was only the shiny black asphalt. If nobody has a car of his own the question of taking a jaunt down the countryside does not arise. The countryside was well cultivated with neat little sleepy villages and it would have been nice to take a drive through them. On both sides of the road from the airport large number of high rise apartment blocks were coming up, some of them finished already. But there was no one to be seen in the windows or around them, no curtains and no clothes to dry. They were empty. The taxis particularly caught his attention. Privatisation of taxi was usually the first step towards capitalism in a communist country. But so many taxis! It was impossible that so many people have gone into the business. He decided to find out and he did. Every driver only smiled and shook his head when asked whether he owned the taxi. On both sides of the road there were lanes for slow moving vehicles. There were a large number of bicycles, a picture so familiar to the outside world. But what was not so familiar was the equally large number of people in very ragged clothes walking down with loads on their heads or on pushcarts or rarely on a donkey cart. The commonest ware were brooms of some sort. These were obviously very poor people but why were they carrying their own wares in a communist country? They were not looking to right or left, not at the roadside open canteens selling cheap food but just trundling down the road monotonously. He was to learn later that these were the lucky villagers from the surrounding villages who had received the permit to enter the city and sell their meagre wares. All this he told me as example of how much you can gather by just looking when I expressed my scepticism about knowing a country by just being there. He told me you have to have the eyes and the thing behind them, known as brain, in active mode. He moved around the city randomly bumping into people and picking up a communication now and then. He was accosted by beggars who were very persistent and pulled him by the sleeves of his jacket for alms. The beggars were all females, some with babies in their arms. He took a picture of a group of beggars in front of a western style hairdressing saloon for ladies, beneath a large billboard of a Japanese multinational. Nobody was going into the shop. At another place he was walking down the road in a tourist area and was surprised to find a high white wall all along one side of the road for quite a long distance. He became curious. What was on the other side of the wall? There were a few small doors in the wall and all of them were closed except one. He went to the open door and peeped through. He was surprised to find the worst possible ghetto with dilapidated thatched roof houses but no human being was in sight. The poor people must have been moved wholesale for developing the place. This would have been very difficult in a democratic society with a free press whether one likes it or not.

In his random wandering one day he bumped into a man he had noticed in the periphery of his working place. He was a handsome young man with proficiency in English—obviously a government functionary. It was his day off. They started talking and with Amol's capacity to put people at ease they soon picked up an intimate conversation. Through him Amol came to know about the human side of communism in China. It was extremely interesting. During Cultural Revolution this man was taken from high school and employed to clean toilets in a remote rural area. His father, an architect, mother, a university professor, elder sister, a post-graduate student, brother, a school student, were similarly treated, all in different corners of the vast country. He has never seen them since. When he came back after it was all over, he had nowhere to stay and he was too old to get into college, which still gave free education. So he worked as an ordinary labourer in one of the many building sites of Beijing and continued his study privately at night, mostly by the street lighting. Eventually he got his graduation from the Open University. With his proficiency in English acquired in the early school days he landed a government job, married and had a daughter, the only one allowed by the State. He now lived in a small house whose small subsidized rent was deducted from his salary. He could not take Amol there, he said. The expenses for his daughter were taken care of by the State and that will include higher education. He could not afford otherwise with his salary of about a hundred dollars a month. He shopped in subsidised government shops, although newly built department stores in Beijing were overflowing with fashionable goods. The prices in these shops were really high. Those were for the businessmen who did not pay taxes, he told with a sneer. He has vacation for two weeks in a year when he takes his family to seaside in a designated area in one of the designated hotels. Amol pointed at his jacket and remarked 'that is an expensive jacket.' The man blushed and said he acquired that on a foreign tour when he went in a delegation with the minister. Everybody wants to go on a foreign tour when you are given a lot of things. Every student in China today dreams of migrating to America or at least to get a job in a multinational company, which can only function as joint ventures in China, he said. Amol asked 'But the Cultural Revolution must have done you some good by integrating the society?' He said 'I do not think so. It has pushed us backward by fifty years. It eliminated all our top intellect.' 'Do you feel bitter?' 'No, not bitter, just sad. What is past is past, life must go on'. 'But today your education is no longer free. As a matter of fact it costs quite a bit compared to what you say is the salary of a well-established person like you. The education of your daughter is free. But what about the countless talented children there must be all over the country to whom that cover is not available? There must be a large number of scholarships and grants.' Amol was thinking of the poor village folk selling their ware. 'Some pay for their own studies. Others must write to Chairman Deng. There are no scholarships as such', was his reply. 'What, thousands, or probably millions must write to Chairman Deng!' 'Yes, he then finds sponsors for them, often from the multinationals.' 'For those who pay, the wages that they can expect to get at the end of their studies does not match the cost of education.' 'Yes, that is true now but we expect newer avenues of income will open up very soon.' And they have opened up for this pragmatic and industrious people.

In his wanderings one day Amol reached the old winter palace of the emperor, now kept as a museum, after having a Chinese type Big Mac from a newly opened McDonald. It was a craze with the youth. After buying tickets and avoiding the souvenir sellers, Amol entered the palace. He noticed that these small entrepreneurs were not as persistent or as professional as in the west and not yet learned to cheat. Even the taxi drivers, the hotel boys did not accept tips, sometimes looked uncomprehendingly when offered. Entering the winter palace he moved from pavilion to pavilion up the hill looking at the exhibits from ancient China. He came to a medium size hall, which contained the legacies from Buddhism, about Buddhism as it came from India. It contained golden statues of ancient gods and goddesses from Mahayana Buddhism—some of them serene, some of them violent and ugly with many hands and heads. Each of them was named and the names were all Indian. There were statues of nine Buddhist monks or Acharyas who were the first to initiate China to Buddhism. Their facial appearance were Chinese but the names were Sanskrit. Amol was overwhelmed. He had known the names of some of the deities and one or two monks, but never knew how they looked or how the Chinese remembered them. It was almost like seeing a page of Indian history in flesh and blood. He wanted to photograph everything in the hall. But there were big signs of 'Photography Prohibited' all around.

Amol looked around and found that a female Red Guard was guarding the hall in her usual dress of navy blue trousers and red jacket. Amol sauntered close to her and saw that she was a young and unusually pretty girl, putting on a grave face as befits a guard. Amol took out his camera and asked for permission in sign language. The girl looked at him severely, pointed at the signboard and wagged her finger, all with as much severity in her face as she could command. Amol moved away but continued to move around the room, looking at the same objects over and over again. Second time he came close to her he had a beseeching look on his face. The girl was still very severe. Amol noticed that she had a chain attached to her jacket button that was probably connected to a whistle. But she was not asking him to leave the pavilion though he must have taken at least three tours around the room for nearly half an hour. Amol thought that in his jeans and sneakers with a designer top he must have been looking much younger than his years and fairly handsome. The girl, even though she was a red guard, must be curious. Amol now chose a moment when the pavilion was empty apart from the two of them and came to the girl again. This time he was really fooling, he said with an embarrassed smile. He started miming and clowning and apparently trying to explain that he was a student whose life depended on taking those pictures and asking for her permission to do so. He even bent down on his knees. The girl kept looking at him severely but there was a smile in her eyes. Gradually the smile spread hovering around the corners of her mouth and then she laughed. It was a very sweet and shy laughter shaking her bobbed black hair and, by a mock order asked him to photograph quickly. She went out of the entrance and stood guard. Amol took his pictures and came out and thanked her profusely. She smiled again. The idea of giving a kiss occurred to him but he desisted, he told me while doubling up with laughter. 'Can you imagine wooing a Red Guard on duty in Communist China? That is the stuff that films are made of. But kissing her was too risky. I did not know how the act of kissing was rated in China. That also varies from country to country. If it was forbidden in China she might have blown the whistle', he said while wiping off tears of laughter from his eyes. 'She was probably a student who could not understand what harm could come to communism by taking pictures of some very antique statues and has probably never seen a 'young' Indian before. I told you they were a pragmatic race.'

The Other China

IT was obvious from Amol's description of his travelogue that he had a great deal of admiration for the Chinese. He would on many occasions praise their ability for hard work, their down to earth attitude to life, the new determination they have acquired. He has often said that this was a civilisation that found most of their own solutions, invented technologies by themselves, removed as they were to one corner of Asia, separated from the rest of the land mass by fearsome deserts and high mountains. They have given more to the world before the modern days than they have taken, from paper to ice cream to gunpowder. I wondered whether it was possible for a race to hold onto its characteristics over several millennia, in spite of changing demands of the time and ever changing political and economic geography. He was of the opinion that the basic traits of a race can lie dormant for long periods of difficult times and flourish when the historical conditions become appropriate. It may look like a new culture but the basic traits remain the same. It was essential, in his opinion, for the ancient civilisations to know their roots and heritage so that the progress in the modern world is orientated in keeping with the traditions for natural and easy acceptance by the masses. He would cite the example of Gandhi. His mass movement was in keeping with the traditions and emotions of India and therefore caught popular imagination. In any other country the same method would have failed and has failed. Similarly, in the case of China the mental attitudes of Maoism and Confucianism are very similar. It was Confucius who had said that the people have a right to forcibly overthrow a king once he has lost the characters that prove his divine mandate to rule. Chinese people have overthrown many kings. Every nation, like individuals, has its strong points in character and the weak ones. An intelligent leadership must evolve policies in keeping with the strength of the nation and guard the weak ones. He also said that China and India are two great ancient civilisations, which are still linked to the past. There is continuity in spite of the changing world, continuity in mental attitude, language. When the world situation becomes favourable they will flourish and mankind will gain a lot. I know he liked what he saw in Communist China though he did not like the subjugation of the individual. He thought this would eventually go. He also thought that a great experiment is on. In India development is being attempted by freeing the individual and in China by subjugating the individual to the State. The future world will see which one was better and the experience will deeply influence the future philosophy of the world. But each country had to find its own solution, its own road to prosperity and creativity. The economic and political theories are only approximations, not sacrosanct in themselves. Therein lies the wisdom of the leadership. I wanted to know whether he found the same Chinese character in the other China, the capitalist Taiwan. Whether a different political and economic philosophy altered the nature of the people. He said that in some respects that was true but not in the basics.

Amol was in Taipei for a short visit. He was sitting at the vast lobby cum bar of a very big hotel idly sipping a drink. He was watching pretty Chinese waitresses with long skirts slit on both sides almost to the waist fleeting noiselessly from table to table. This was something, he thought, not to be found in Communist China. A large contingent of businessmen from Japan had just come in. As they were checking in, pretty young Chinese girls were coming in and getting introduced and attached to each man. It seemed to be all pre-arranged as part of the visit as if it came with the air ticket from the travel agent. Perhaps it did. There was no hustle and bustle, just quiet arrangement. There were no hugs or kisses, no endearing addresses, they just picked up their briefcases and their girls and went off to their rooms. Humourously Amol made a mental note for a future comparative study of the sexual habits of the oriental and the occidental. He had seen similar businessmen in Communist China. If they had such facilities there it was not so overtly visible. In any case, when you were shown into your room by a bellboy you were not asked whether you needed a girl. In Taipei Amol was asked by a huge janitor who almost looked like a bouncer.

At workplace everything was efficient and cool. The Chinese were serious and efficient in work but liked to enjoy their evenings. In Communist China there was very little opportunity for that. In Taipei there was plenty. Amol expressed his desire to sample the Chinese way of eating snakes. One of his fixed ideas was to taste local delicacies. He said that you could not know a people without tasting their food and understanding it. And when you do that you come closest to their heart. He was taken to a small street known as snake alley. There were small restaurants on both sides and all of them served snake dishes. The snakes were kept in large wooden crates at the entrance. You chose your snake as you went in. The snake was taken out, hung by its neck from a rope and its chest was cut open. The main artery from the heart was cut and the blood poured into a glass half filled with a strong local rice wine. As you drank, the snake was cooked in the way you wanted. Amol told me that, though he did not have any prejudices about food, this was the only time he balked at trying a new dish. There were special shops dealing only in poisonous snakes, some types of vipers, and it cost a fortune to have a viper. The Chinese thought that eating snakes and drinking the blood increased their virility and a lot of the customers were old men. Amol's friend Peter was egging him on. 'Come on, be brave, have a snake.' Amol said 'Why don't you go ahead and show the way.' 'I do not need it' said Peter. 'Neither do I.' Raw snake blood was the one thing in the world that Amol could not take.

He had a young hostess at his workplace whose name was Ruby. Amol raised his eyebrows when she introduced herself and asked whether that was a Chinese name. She said it was not but the Chinese name was too difficult to pronounce. Amol said 'Cut out the American crap. We have pronounced each other's name for thousands of years.' She said her name was Jin Jiang. Amol always called her by that name. When his project was coming to an end she told him one day while serving coffee, 'Do you know that you are very handsome.' Amol said unmindfully 'is that so?' Another day at coffee time she said 'our island nation is very beautiful. There are beautiful places to see. Why don't you take a few days' leave after the work is finished and rent a car? I shall take you around and show you beautiful places. It will only take a few days.' Amol smiled, took her hands and said 'It would have been lovely. But I have to save some money since I promised my wife that I shall take her to Europe for holiday next month.'

I could not help saying 'you really have a way with women, don't you? I do not know how many heads you have turned and left them in the lurch. That is not very manly, is it?' He laughed 'what do you mean? If I accommodated all of them I do not know where I would be today.' Then he became serious. 'Well, you are partly right. I adore women and they instinctively know it when you do that. They are more natural, more gracious and kinder than men. They have given me a lot throughout my life in different ways. But that is probably because I have always found the right kind of women, my kind of women, corresponding to my centre of love. Otherwise they can be pain in the neck, as bad as men. Be honest with them and they will give you everything. This, of course, I am saying as a man. I do not know how a woman in my situation feels. Sex generalisations are risky now-a-days.

But I can tell you that my spectrum is indeed very large, with a large variety of customs and emotions. I have enjoyed it much more without sex. Do not think I suppressed myself. I was always more concerned about violating their sincerity than their body. May be the opportunity was there once or twice that I passed over without realizing or for not wanting it. I do not regret it because they have given me a lot, a depth of insight into human nature that I would not have had otherwise. Lust does not give you that. Trying seduction and sex might have spoilt it all. I have known men who have made a habit of it and call it a conquest. Their lives have seemed sterile to me. How can you give all of yourself to every woman you like or adore and if you cannot give what do you gain? I shall tell you another story, a story at once funny and sad. I promise you this will be my last story on the subject of women. We shall slowly grow up.'

The Girl from Dhaka

AMOL was once catching a British Airways flight from Bangladesh. He flew in to the Dhaka international airport in the morning and his connection was in the afternoon. So he had a few hours to spend at the airport. He was travelling economy. The transit lounge was a bare long hall with rows of chairs and a television set at one end. There was nothing else, no bar, and no restaurant. Amol decided to sit it out with a book and skip the lunch. There was only one other occupant of the hall. This was a female who seemed to be of humble origin. She sat mostly on the floor with her tied down cloth baggage. She had her head covered, a devout Muslim. At the time of mid-day namaz she had a wash, spread a sheet on the floor and did her namaz. Until then they had not exchanged any words. She now looked at Amol and asked in Urdu where he was going. Amol gave his destination. She said she was waiting for a flight to Lahore, which was before Amol's. Still sitting on the floor she opened her baggage and brought out food packages. She opened some of them and brought out home made chapatis and some other things. She asked Amol whether he would like some food. He was hungry, he had to pass the time and he wanted to keep up the acquaintance. She intrigued him. She was not very young but not very old either. She had a serene and pious face. She could have humble origins but could also have a noble background. Now that she talked, it was hard to tell. She fed Amol with care offering him more. She herself ate after that. Amol was reminded of the story of Lady Fatima. But however much he tried he could not get her to talk about herself, as to who she was or what she did. It was one of the rare failures of Amol. When the time came she picked up her bags and walked out of the hall. To this day Amol regretted that he did not carry her bags to the check-in desk and see whether she actually checked in or vanished in thin air. She seemed so elusive.

Amol boarded his flight and a number of passengers from Bangladesh were boarding too. Among that crowd Amol's attention was drawn to a tall young girl wearing a salwar-kameez. The girl was not particularly beautiful but what attracted his attention was her dress, which was of a peculiar shiny material. More than the material the shape and cut of the dress was such that it would be considered dowdy, rustic or provincial by a modern Indian girl. All other women in the group were wearing saris. Not only her dress, but also the open sandals on her feet were looking incongruous as she was going west in late autumn. Her height had possibly given her a little stoop, faint but noticeable. Here was a girl who obeyed. But she was otherwise quite amiable, talking to a number of people in the group in a familiar manner, friends probably or relatives. As was Amol's habit, he was building up a total mental picture of the person from appearance, as he had nothing better to do. In the process their eyes met several times and the girl noticed that he was watching her.

On reaching Heathrow Amol moved into the transit area and sometime later noticed that the girl, with some of her companions, was also in transit. He had to wait a few hours for his connection. He took out a book and in between reading was idly watching the group from Bangladesh. One of the men in the group smiled at him and after some time came over to him obviously wanting to chat a little. They were also curious. The Bangladeshi man was a lawyer travelling on some errand. He talked about Islamic power. He said that the Iran Iraq war, which was then going on, was just eyewash and was aimed at arming Iraq and testing the weapons and the troops. The world would know its real effect in near future was what he said. Amol was puzzled. All that killing and bloodshed were only eyewash, he wondered. Do the people know it? The man said that does not matter, this was the only way to get at the West. The power of Islam would be revealed. The man left him after some time. Amol kept on wondering about what he said. Even if the story was not true, so much hatred, when they were still living on the dole, was so disturbing. The history was to show that the man was telling the truth and Amol puzzled even now. How come the lawyer from Bangladesh knew the mind of Iraq when other countries, at least publicly, knew nothing about it? He thought that if this trend went on, the world would have to fear Islam in future.

Amol concentrated on his book again. Shortly afterwards he was startled out of his reverie by a female voice. The girl he had been noticing since Dhaka was at his side and asking for permission to sit down beside him. She had a melodious voice. As this was a double couch, Amol made space for her to sit down. The girl took out a book from her purse and opened it on her lap though she had no intention of reading. She asked him where he was coming from and where he was going. Amol told her. She asked his name. Amol gave her the name. In any case it was written on his handbag. She asked 'You are a Hindu?' Amol nodded. She gave him her name. Let us say it was Meena. Bangladeshi girls and boys of her generation often had a Hindu nickname after their Muslim name, which made it sound very sweet to Amol. This was a very welcome change after the militant lawyer. They chatted about the common language and literature, about the war of independence of Bangladesh, about many common cultures and customs, laughed about some of the shared jokes. Looking at close quarters the dress did not seem so cheap after all, but the sandal was intriguing. Amol asked about her destination and whether she was travelling in a group. She said she was travelling alone and others were only fellow travellers whom she met at the airport. She was going to Montreal. As politely as he could Amol asked the purpose of her visit. She said she was going to meet her husband. Amol said that was a very welcome journey. The girl said, 'I am going for the first time. We have been married only a few months back'. Amol congratulated her and wished her good luck and also joked about what a honeymoon it will be. The girl's eyes misted over. She said 'I do not even know him' and was silent. Amol asked her 'But you must have seen him at the time of marriage'. She said 'Hardly. He was gone the next day'. Amol could now see the terror in her eyes as the tears welled up. She was silent and still looking at the book on her lap. Amol felt a wave of sympathy. It was clear during their conversation that she knew very little English, if at all. He placed his hand over hers holding the book and gave a little squeeze. 'Everything will turn out to be good, you'll see' he said to console her. 'Men often do not marry in the land of their domicile and like to have a wife from home. They can share more that way'. The girl now broke down. With suppressed sobs she let go of the book on her lap and grabbed his hand in her two hands. Amol gently asked 'What does he do?' 'He works in a restaurant' she said. Then she said the most improbable thing 'Why don't you take me with you? I do not want to go to him. Take me wherever you are going.' Amol was taken aback. He looked up and surveyed the vast transit lounge. Was he travelling in the twentieth century through a modern civilisation or was he in the middle of the Arabian Nights? This was crazy. It can't be true. In less than twenty-four hours he had met Lady Fatima, then the marauding Turko Mongol fanatical warrior and then this half-veiled beauty with kohl smeared burning eyes on a camel back. He was seeing the whole Islamic culture in one go. He rubbed his eyes with his free hand. The girl was still hanging on to the other. He told her as gently as he could 'you are going to Canada and I am going to USA. You do not have a US visa. Apart from everything else you just cannot go there. You do not know me and I know nothing of you. These are not fairytale days.' But she just kept on repeating the same thing through their now desultory conversation. The girl by this time was sitting very close holding his left hand with both her hands. She snuggled even closer. The physical closeness was getting really uncomfortable but the girl did not mind. To a casual observer it would have seemed that two lovers were sitting together. Amol was conscious of that and very uncomfortable but the girl was oblivious. She seemed to be in a trance playing with his fingers. Fortunately, the Montreal flight was announced. Barring one or two of her countrymen, others had left by this time in other flights. Amol told her that she had to board her plane now. She did not seem to hear but kept sitting in the same pose silently. Eventually the last call was announced. Amol told her 'That was the last call, you have to go.' Reluctantly she got up, picked up her bag and sauntered out through the darkened hallway. A much-relieved Amol relaxed in his seat. His flight was still another hour away. He heard the boarding call for Montreal. He kept looking at the dark corridor through which the girl had gone thinking about her, about the figure with the slight stoop, resignation written all over her. Then to his great surprise and horror he saw the girl coming back. He became afraid of a scene and who knows what shape it would take. Maybe she had left something. He looked around. There was nothing. The girl was coming straight at him, her face fixed in a trance. The final urgent call of boarding for Montreal was announced. The girl came straight for him but was not looking at him. Her face still fixed in a trance, she came to him, circled round his seat twice without looking at him, without looking for anything she might have dropped and then walked back into the dark corridor, never to return again.

Amol was silent. Then he looked up and asked 'Can you tell me why she came back? I have never been able to fathom it. I can still sometimes see her walking into that corridor as if into a cave, with a village girl's walk and a hopeless surrender written all over her. I know it is not uncommon in our sub-continent to make friends on a long journey and even to pour out very personal anguish and secrets to someone whom one does not expect to meet a second time. I can also allow for a bit of flirting that is not uncommon, but this was too much.' I had no answer. I have never heard such things happening to anybody I know. I ventured 'May be you exude some sort of extrasensory spiritual power sometimes, which touches people in despair.' He shot back 'Don't talk rubbish.' Then as if to himself he went on talking 'I have met people from Bangladesh, both boys and girls. I have met them in Bangladesh and in other countries. They are a very direct and daring people. In general, I like them though some people find them crude. The girls are usually pretty and they have an aura of sophistication, which is peculiar to

Muslim women of all social status even though it is the same people on both sides of the border. I have seen Bangladeshi boys in Germany who come in and burn their passports. They manage to live on dole for some time and if they cannot get a permanent foothold in Germany or elsewhere in Europe, they save enough money to fly to Bahamas where you did not need a passport in those days. I do not know about now. From Bahamas in ordinary boats they cross the ocean to get to USA. Many of them die at sea. The world does not know about them. The media watches only the Cubans. In this fashion they have been spreading all over the world. I really admire their courage and enterprise.' I said that the hard life in Bangladesh was probably the driving force. He thought that alone does not explain it entirely. There has to be an element of adventure and enterprise. That sort of emigration happened in India a long time back but it is no longer there.

I asked 'You have also been to Pakistan, have you not?' He said 'Oh, yes. I like the people. They are the same people as in north-west India really. A Punjabi on either side of the border has more in common than with a Bengali, as history has proved. Even in modern days it is the similar people who fight the bitterest wars. Look at England and Germany, North Ireland, the Jews and the Palestinians, Serbs, Croats and Bosnians, Indians and Pakistanis and so many others. Perhaps it is the end of *Kaliyug*, end of our times, when brothers kill brothers. I once told a powerful politician of Pakistan that you allow *Vedanta* to enter Pakistan. Let people study the Holy Quran and Vedanta together and discern and discuss. I shall love to say the same thing to the Prime Minister of India if I have the chance. When the people learn to have trust and confidence in each other's life philosophy and develop mutual respect the political problems will become less. You cannot pass over religion nor push it under the carpet. Let a world religion evolve, discerning the profound from the temporal in each religion, and let it come into force. He told me that I was talking of profound things that are not practical. But looking at the world and its madness don't you feel that the time has come to talk of profound things? Nothing else will bring sanity. Such nice people in India and Pakistan, they should learn to control their fanatical fringe and realise that the days of fanaticism are over. I feel the women have a much greater role to play in this regard than the men. That is why I admire them. It is the women who bear the first brunt of fanaticism in every religion. Let us help them reject and revolt.'

I said: 'You have been out of this sub-continent for a long time. That is probably why you have such an open and liberal view of Islam, out of the turmoil.'

He said: 'Oh no, I have always held these views. I have many Muslim friends in this country and abroad. Historically Islam has two faces, almost a split personality. On one side there is great piety, humanism, spirituality and intellect. On the other there is extreme fanaticism and cruelty. The second part is probably a later add on from the days of Turkish invasion and Mongol sacking of Baghdad. The problem to the outside world is that they do not know which face will be turned on when. The problem is also inside the Muslim society. But, I think, if the world goes on, they will find the balance and will come to see that they have much more to gain with their humanism than with fanaticism. This is true not only for Islam but also for all the major world religions. After all in this modern age of science, if there is a God, there can be only one.'

The Dialogue

THE dusk had fallen and along with it came the mosquitoes. We had to shift indoors. We carried our drinks, bottles and glasses and made ourselves cozy. I was thinking about Amol's stories. As was the custom, we had a few hours before the call for supper. We wrapped ourselves in shawls and sat cross-legged on the low divan. As I was ruminating on the stories our discussion followed the same line. This is a dialogue of which I have kept notes after he left and I shall present it as such.

I: From your stories it appears that where women are concerned, religion does not matter to you.

Amol: That is unkind. I do not make any discrimination among men on the ground of religion either.

I: Be that as it may, it would seem from your stories that you made love to women with your head only. You have no experience of sensual pleasures. Is it something you are putting on for me or is this real?

Amol laughed, 'You mean to ask whether I have had or capable of having carnal pleasures. I have to put it on record for you that I have had enough experience, at least enough for me. They often end in sadness or apathy and the stories are nothing to write home about. I do not know whether you will agree with me, but I think, that when you are indulging in sex without your mind or your love in it, psychologically it is equivalent to masturbation. That is not a story. One thing that I have not had enough of and probably never will is love.

I: And pray tell me what that is.

Amol: I never thought when we started this evening that you would drag me into this difficult discussion of which I do not know whether I have a clear picture. In any case let me try. It seems to me that we have a centre for love in our brain. It may not be a solitary centre but a combination of several. What I mean is that there is a prototype in our brain. I do not want to enter into the old romantic argument whether love is subjective or objective. In today's permissive world it is obvious to everybody that each one of us love to love a certain type of individual who may be similar or dissimilar to us. That means we carry the idea of a prototype in our head and we love the specimens that match that idea. It is not simply the pheromone but something far more complicated. And this matching, consciously or unconsciously, goes on throughout life. We rejoice at every find but nothing is a complete fit. In other words, with every incomplete match we are titillating only our own centre, our own mind. This is not just sex. In fact this is sometimes at odds with sex bringing in unhappiness. This unhappiness is also unreal if we realise that what we are in love with is the idea of love inside ourselves. How does this idea form? It must need a lot of inputs. But at the centre there must be something, like a hardware, which is original that takes in the inputs, the software. Like everybody else I also will never have enough of these close matches. The only difference is that unlike most people I am a conscious participant. I know that ultimately what I am loving is myself. This is true not only in relation to the female sex but a lot of other things. Am I clear?

I: You call this clear? The thing you are describing is beyond my comprehension. It seems that this love of yours finds sex as an unwanted but inevitable impediment, at least sometimes. And the love within one's own self, is this not selfish or narcissistic?

Amol: How can it be selfish or narcissistic when you are giving it to others? You are only giving the best you have. You are also misquoting me on sex. I do not decry sex. How can I? Sex is the first great awareness in human life. With its advent at puberty our entire psyche changes. We become aware of the world around us, of our own self and our environment. With it comes kindness, love, the feeling of wonder, creativity and spirituality. Have you ever pondered over the closeness of spirituality and sexuality? Spirituality has great sexual attraction and all old spiritual religious orders keep their novices cloistered. With puberty we become conscious of our body, of the conflict of our mind and body. God, or shall I say evolution, has made a practical joke with humankind. He has placed the head of God on the body of an animal and puberty marks the great awakening of both. That is probably what the Sphinx depicts. Those ancient cultures might have been low on knowledge but were great in perception. Sex works as the great awakening, but it also works as the great veil, along with its accompaniments like lust, greed, hatred, power, possessions, corruption and ambition. But love also rises and that rises in the head. We are creatures of biology. We are very possessive about those loves and joys that come out of our biological life connected to the emotions of biological existence. We also experience another kind of love and joy that we love to share, like music, works of art, spirituality etc. There we are actually coming out of our narrow possessive self. We are actually forgetting ourselves. Why should we find joy in forgetting the self? Those works of art that we say have passed the test of time do this to great many of us beyond great expanses of time and space with no scientific reason or proof apart from the fact that a lot of people have experienced the same. We treasure them as the great gifts of humanity. Actually, if you think about it, a major part of our life consists of these experiences where we are not entirely behaving like a naked ape. It is in all of us in one form or another, even to the tone deaf, the ignorant in art. Even sex can be elevated, or should I say changed, to this level but it is difficult.

I: You seem to admire celibacy. Do you mean to say that celibacy is the only way to make whatever it is in the head to grow?

Amol: Who am I to give a prescription or to judge and, for that matter, who can be the judge but one's own self? Celibacy cannot be forced on somebody just as philandering cannot be forced. It is pointless to prescribe or judge these things. I respect celibacy and true celibacy is hard to achieve, but not impossible. Celibacy has to be in the mind and not in the body alone. It is not a wilful suppression or avoidance of sex but not having a desire for it or its vicarious accompaniments like lust, greed, hatred, love of power, ambition etc. Celibacy is not abnormal or unphysiological as sex oriented sections of the society or some psychologists would make us believe. A strong willed suppression can be self-defeating, but not true celibacy. True celibacy can only be achieved with total intellectual development. That is why when I find true celibacy I bow my head because I know that behind it there is a high intellect and perception even if it is not apparent at a first glance. But even a partial celibacy is good for health so long it is not forceful or put up. Celibacy ideally means that one has to be celibate from birth. But it is good even if it is acquired later. You do not have to show it off or experiment with it or tell it to others, you just know it within yourself. It gets rid of a lot of trouble. But I really detest the experimenters; there may be something phony there.

I: I have not heard of this type of intellect. What is it and how do you acquire it?

Amol: Why do you call it a different type of intellect? It is not. Take for example a scientist, a physicist for example. He studies a lot of physics through school and college and commits a lot of things to memory. If his brain remains restricted to whatever he has studied and committed to memory, will he ever make a new discovery? For that to happen he has to go beyond what he has learned and try for new insight and perception. It is this same thing I am talking about. You have to have an education, through studies and experience, as extensive as possible and then transcend it to ponder on things beyond. Even pondering over science will do, or over music or literature or, like me, you can ponder and meditate over life's experiences with total detachment and honesty. That last thing, which I do, all of us can do. It is possible for ordinary men like us to take this path and then you feel the bliss and the beauty of having this something in the head, as you call it. You have to go beyond sex and its accompaniments, beyond knowledge and beyond intellect and religion, as we usually understand it. I do not have a word for that. But you do not necessarily suffer all of the obstacles. Human life is too short for that. You suffer one or two and then switch on to something, if you are lucky, and then arrive somewhere that I cannot define.

I: I get a vague idea. But this intellectualisation of sex is too much. Do you think this had something to do with Britt going away? Have you ever met her in all these years?

Amol smiled: You are a devil. You wouldn't let go on anything. You know perfectly well that I had to go back. But, as for Britt, human actions are seldom, if ever, motivated by a single cause or event. I do not think that is the reason why Britt went away. In fact she never went away. Our lives just flowed in different directions. But yes I went back, I had to. I was missing her very badly. It was not a physical void, but a lot more. It puzzled me. I was upset and frustrated that one person should have so much control over my emotions, of my whole being. I went back after nearly ten years. This was just before she would go away into wilderness. She invited me to dinner at her apartment, just the two of us. She cooked herself, laid out the dinner beautifully. It was very nice. We chatted before and through the dinner about people we knew, about old times. It was so congenial; the vibes was so good that we were transported to ten years back. The time literally stood still. After dinner we were lolling on the sofa relaxing and having coffee and still talking. I told her that it seemed time had not moved. Should we make love for old times sake? She smiled and said no, but asked me to stay the night or as long as I could. I was already married then and of course she knew it. I remembered our intense passions and tried to rouse her, I suppose as much her as myself. We knew each other's moves very well. It only resulted in a lot of laughter and fun but nothing else. Then she told me that she had to talk to me and ask my opinion about something. I was the only person in her world whom she could ask. The tone was serious. She brought out a photograph of a man whom we both knew and were fond of. The only surprise was that in the photo he was bare bodied above the waist. I asked when it was taken. She said not very long ago. I waited. After a long wait she said that she wanted to go away with him but was not able to make up her mind. 'I have always liked him, always been fond of him. You also knew that. Don't tell me you didn't know.' I told her yes I knew and we were both fond of him. But what did she mean by going away, where? I knew the man loved wilderness, used to roam around alone whenever he could, but he was also much older, about double our age even at that time. She said she wanted to go away with him, to the wilderness, never to return. There was no reason to return any more. I asked about his family, a family he was fond of. She said that the children had grown up and gone their own ways and he had divorced his wife. I asked whether she would marry him. She said 'No, I don't want to marry him. Marriage brings a lot of problems. I could have married you, in fact wanted to. But you never proposed.' I was surprised. The question of marriage never came up between us. I was not ready for marriage and never thought of it. I told her so. She said she knew, but still hoped. I said 'But you never even mentioned.' She put a finger on my lips and smiled 'you have not grown up even now, just as dumb as ever. A girl does not talk of such things.' I remembered with some fondness that 'dumbo' was her favourite nickname for me. I said I still did not see what was making her go away to the arctic wilderness but it certainly was a long way off from the hot humid and crowded cities where she would have probably lived had we married. I asked her why not live together in the city or wherever he was. She said it was the same thing really and a lot worse than marriage. There were laws for that too. No, she wanted to go away from it all. 'Having a man around is useful, you know, and especially if you like him' she winked at me. There was so much she had to learn, like fishing under the icy crust of the sea or lakes, how to gather food, how to fend off danger. I asked her what advice she needed. She said just this much, whether she should marry him and settle in the city or go away together to the wilderness. Marrying somebody and then going off to the jungle was a silly idea. He was eager for the jungle but could compromise. She had to make up her mind.

There was a long pause. At last I asked 'What advice did you give?'

He awoke as if from a long dream and looked at me 'Are you mad? Why should I give an advice? Do you think people need advice when they want to go away? She was only sounding it against me, a human being who liked and loved both of them, who will not make it into a scandal or may be it was something else I did not know. I do not know whether I had anything to do with it or may be I had, who knows. I was puzzled. There was no pain, only a puzzle. But it is very difficult for us sometimes to analyse our own feelings. You may have an ulcer pain and think that it was hunger. The puzzle was so intense along with a sense of guilt that I had to go back a third time and a fourth time. She had already left. Last time I went I was with my wife and two kids. It was the same place minus Britt. We drove around and ran around the same streets, ate hot dogs with mash in similar roadside stalls, drove through forests, had coffee under the pine and birch, visited the same restaurants. The children particularly were so excited that they gave me a feeling of immensity of time, of a motion through space where every little bit mattered but nothing mattered in isolation. Nothing, nothing happened to me. I was free at last. My wife loved it, my kids loved it and we were all very happy. Looking back I do not think I went with any deliberate intention of purging myself. The journey was not planned that way. It just happened, as is the case with many things in our lives. The laws of causality have a very queer way of working. It works in a rational way only in fiction. With Britt also it probably just happened. She is still there and she is alone now.'

We were silent for a long time staring into the night. At last I said 'You should have married her.'

Amol was startled out of his reverie and laughed 'and complete the story for you? The story never ends Horatio, it just goes on.' And he laughed again. 'You do not see the story going on all around you? It is going on all around the earth, all around the universe, all around you. Can't you see? It is the finiteness of man that ends the stories. What is relevant in one time and space is not relevant in another but the story goes on. Rise above time and space and look beyond, if you can stand it; open your third eye and you will see. The indeterminacy, the chaotic chance that is in the universe, the indeterminacy that is between the quantum description of the microcosm and the classical description of the macrocosm, that indeterminacy is also in you. You are a creature of the universe and the universe is in your head as much as it is out there. Rise above it and your mind may blow out, but feel it and be content.'

I said, 'All these perceptions came to you by the trauma that was Britt?'

Amol said, 'You are incurable. You shall have to satisfy your ideas of causality, your enquiring mind. As I have already told you no single event determines action or thought, if you analyse it that way. You pass through life rubbing against people and events. Each one gives you a little charge. It all builds up to a level and gives a spark and your whole life transforms because you start seeing things in a different way. Outwardly there is no change. I shall tell you what happened. What I am telling you came to me gradually much later, not at the time, or even during my last visit. Britt was part of a space-time. Separate the two and the whole thing changes colour. Our life goes through a series of space-time areas like the rest of the universe but only for a very short time compared to the universe. Qualitatively it is the same. We can perceive time flowing but we cannot perceive space flowing. Each time I was going back I was not really going back to the same place, though geographically it was the same place. Because we do not understand space we have so much difficulty to understand the Theory of Relativity. Even today many of its postulates are only understood through mathematics but we cannot feel them or comprehend them as solid experiences. In the special circumstances of Britt, the space-time was a capsule. Therefore it was possible to understand it, though much later. I have often wondered that we are born and in time we die. But do we die in space also? It is an interesting thought; you must agree to that. Do we go to a different space? In that case we shall have to leave our body behind, we cannot take all that clutter. If we leave our body behind what do we take? I do not know the answer to that, but I have certainly left a little bit of my mind in the space-time capsule that had Britt in it. But there is no sense of loss. Why should there be no sense of loss when something is taken from an entity? It is because the laws of mathematics do not operate here.'

I said, 'If I may be permitted to say so, the whole story of Britt can be described easily in a more colloquial way than going into all that high philosophy. Why are you going into such high gear? Is it necessary for survival?'

Amol said 'All the profundities of life can also be fitted into the ordinary. In fact ordinary is not really ordinary, like the falling of an apple. The simplest things hold the deepest secrets. It is like Newton's science and Einstein's science. Everything fitted so nicely in Newtonian science except only one or two odd ones. People should have been happy with that and lived with it, but they were not. It was only a handful of people who were unhappy. But trying to fit those few odd things altered the whole structure of science and human thought and our mind. How do you explain that? Since then science is progressing at an even faster pace, from known to unknown, from determinacy to indeterminacy and who knows what beyond. Do you not think that such progress is possible and desirable in human affairs, even in a single human being? Is it not necessary to integrate the creatures that are making this progress, with science itself? Is it not necessary to ponder over what sort of logic should apply to man and his emotions and perceptions? Is Aristotelian logic, the logic of science enough for that? What logic should define love beyond satisfaction of biological needs, the rapture of Beethoven's symphony?' Then he smiled 'in this world, Horatio, the sublime and the ridiculous are often inextricably intertwined. It is for you to disentangle them and rejoice. After all what is in life but to rejoice. Rejoice, brother, rejoice, the church bells are ringing. Oh, how I wish that your name were Horatio. I have already made two quotable quotes. I could even become immortal.'

I was pensive, thoughtful. I have never thought of things this way. I cannot entirely grasp what he was saying but neither could I discount the whole thing as rubbish. I was in half a trance. Was he hypnotising me? I could only utter 'Can you make apples fly?'

He burst out laughing. "May be I can, I do not know. But why should I want to do that? It will completely destabilise your life. If you want to do it, try yourself. Do not ask me to show you. But seriously speaking, can't you see the constants around us falling down one after the other like dominoes? First to go was time followed by the position of electron and now the speed of light is almost going. What would be next, maybe the value of pi? Supposing they all went in one go before we understood them, say about four hundred years back, what would have happened? Mankind probably would have gone back to the jungle, would have given up. Bringing it all in small doses is good for health and for growth of perception. The life of an individual is also a fragment of humankind and behaves in the same way. Ask a man on the street what all this means to him, this falling down of constants and he will say 'nothing'. But you and I know better and keep it to us. He will believe when we take him on an intergalactic journey at one blink of his eyelids."

I was still in a trance. I said, 'How do you do it!'

He was puzzled. 'What do you mean?'

I said 'How do you realise so much?'

He was relaxed again. 'Oh that? You have to do it yourself old man. Nobody can teach—not Jesus, not Buddha, not The Prophet Muhammad, not Spinoza and Kant, not *Vedanta*—you have to do it all by yourself. They can only show you the way, but you have to do it all by yourself. You are a lone traveller. But I can tell you that *Vedanta* shows only the way and promises nothing else. Others show you a goal, even make material promises and as a result the goal is often confused. They have been cluttered too much by the vicissitudes of the human history. If you use a staff of pure gold as a plough or as a sword for some temporal gain, you shall deform it. *Vedanta* remains uncluttered, as it promises nothing, never having delivered the goodies, at least in the known time. Because, there is nothing to deliver, nothing to win except your own self. The whole thing is for you to see and realise.'

I relaxed for the first time. 'Oh, so it was your background. But in your story telling you have never once touched India. Have you never received any inspiration from the land you were born in?'

Amol said, 'Oh yes, much indeed. But these things know no geographic boundary, no boundaries of religion. They spread out a long time back. They are in the consciousness of men, I mean women too. In modern Indian society there is very little of real value. You have to dig really deep down to get something of value. But still, India is very much in my psyche; I cannot deny that. Modern Indian society is a hybrid society. The rough edges of intellectualism had died down a thousand years back. Poverty and forced conformity had almost killed the society. It is rejuvenating for only a hundred and fifty years. The surprising thing is that it has still got its own fires deep down, fires from a civilisation five thousand years old or may be more, who knows. Western civilisation has been lighting this eerie silted landscape for the last two hundred years and may be revealing more of its ugliness. But in this psychedelic vista the society is throwing up its gems for the world to absorb. The gems are of real value. Whether one day they will cover the world is for others to tell. I can only tell you a few stories because I am only a storyteller. The stories will tell you, a no non-sense man of the world, whether they are only in my psyche or they have a concrete existence of their own. I am not a judge and not a participant; I do not play for any of the teams. You want me to retrace my steps to the roots of my mind. It is a difficult task. But let me not come into it right now. Let me go around it a bit and see it from the outside. India is better viewed from outside, so also one's roots.'

I interjected before he could start his new story. 'So in all your restless roaming you were really trying to find India, find your roots?'

He thought for some time and then said 'You are partly right there. I think I was trying to find myself but not just in the background of India. I was trying to find myself in the background of the world. Let me bring in a simile. You were fond of classical music. You still are? Yes you are. Then it is easy. When you listen to the Western classical music what happens in your mind, what gladdens you? It is the harmony that transports you beyond your selfish self. A hundred piece orchestra working out a great melody in complete harmony. Every piece is perfect and together they bring out a harmonious melody, the melody of the universe, the stars dancing, the galaxies rotating and me this little self is a part of it all. It is the external harmony. There may be a lead player or a soloist but it is still more or less the same. When you listen to the Indian classical music what happens in the mind? You hear the individual striving of a sitar, sarod or flute player to rise gradually to a perfection, to build up gradually as far as he can go to a supersensory level to build up the same resonance in you, to a complete harmony within himself and in you, the internal harmony. It is like the striving of a soul and the musician actually keeps on innovating within his boundaries and from his knowledge as he goes along. It is usually accompanied by another instrument, sometimes it is another musical instrument but more often by a percussion instrument, like a tabla. But the two instruments are not playing at the same time; they are working in tandem. When the sitar is in ascendant the tabla is playing quietly and *vice versa*. The percussion is vital to the attainment of perfection, like the dance of Shiva as he plays the *Damaru*, a sort of two in one Bongo drums and the whole music is a duality. Those of us who understand both types of music are really fortunate. One is creating harmony in combination and the other is creating quest and rise to harmony of an individual. Such music is really a reflection of the cultures. One is creating harmony of the multiple, harmony of the society and the other is creating quest for harmony of an individual, harmony of the self. The two are inseparable, you cannot have one without the other. There have been attempts at fusing the two types of music but it does not work. You cannot fuse with your mirror image but you can have two equally good arms. That is what drives me. I love them both and I try to find myself between my two arms. Interestingly enough many great Indian classical musicians are Muslims and the fusion of Hindu and Muslim cultures is complete in the field of Indian classical music. This is because it is a matter of perception. Do I make myself clear what I am striving at? I really do love them both and I do not like forced fusion because the internal and external worlds, though related, are different.'

The India Abroad

AMOL went to Bali for a conference. Indonesia always held a deep fascination for him. He told me that here was a cauldron for fusion of cultures but it was geographically isolated enough for the fusion to mature without repeated invasions as in India. He wanted to sample the product first hand. He had Indonesian friends. He had also had short stays on job. But this time he was determined to take time off and see.

The island of Bali is fascinating and very easy to see. It is a small island that you can cover completely in a car in two or three days. Bali is a miniature world with miniature super highways, miniature cities and villages, miniature mountain ranges, jungles, sea beaches and even its miniature volcano. It is like a children's playground. He drove out one day from the miniature western pleasure spot at Nusa Dua with its large hotels, beaches with usual sports, conference rooms, dance halls and all other paraphernalia of a synthetic culture to see real Bali. For three days he roamed every nook and corner, talking to endless people, sometimes in English, sometimes in sign language and sometimes in snatches of Sanskrit. The Vasa Indonesia had as much its roots in Sanskrit as his own and older people spoke a dialect which was recognisable. He went to Jogjakarta in Java but no further, as on that trip he was not interested in modernity. He did not describe his experiences as in a travelogue but as his impressions of its culture and people. The experiences were so profound and so dear that he has decided never to go back again lest that golden picture gets sullied. He would rather love the golden girl of Rabindranath Tagore that he has also seen and fallen in love with.

The first place he stopped on his way as he drove was at a place called Batubulan. He entered a Batik factory with its own showroom. It was lunch break hour. The girls working at the factory were resting. He entered the darkened showroom and loitered around. One by one the curious girls came in. They asked him what he wanted. He looked at things and made desultory enquiries. It was clear he had no intention to buy and with a shy smile at last he confessed that he only wanted to talk to them. The girls burst out laughing, held his hands and said 'OK, then let us talk.' They took him to a sitting place and thronged around with curiosity. They asked his nationality and he said he was an Indian. 'Are you a Hindu', they asked. He said 'yes', and that did it. They sat down around him as if they had found a long lost relative. The girls were in their twenties with the curiosity and innocence of that age. They made him sit down and asked him to stay for the day. He talked to each of them by turn; asked where they lived, the family members, how long they worked, what they did. They had finished school and some of them could speak English fairly well. Those who could, translated for others. Some of the girls were pretty but all of them were healthy and well turned out. Making Batik is a delicate artwork and woman's job and these girls worked in two shifts. Their exquisite and expensive craft on silk and cotton needed a lot of discipline and concentration and that culture was visible. The atmosphere became very congenial. Amol told them they were very pretty. They rolled in laughter and said 'Oh, come off, the Indian girls are so pretty.' Amol asked 'Have you seen many Indian girls?' 'We have seen in films' was their reply. Amol asked them whether they were married. 'No' they said. One girl, the smartest of them, looked around at others with a quizzical smile and said 'But all of us have one, what do you call it, a boy friend?' Amol gave a sigh of great disappointment 'All?' There was another peal of laughter. By now they were all great friends. Amol asked them how they start their day, when they come to the workshop, how did they learn such fine handiwork. The Batik was of a very fine quality not found elsewhere. Its artistry was exquisite and was very expensive. He asked 'Do you do any prayer or worship before you start work? The things that you do must need a lot of concentration and steady hands.' One girl replied 'Yes we chant a hymn on getting up in the morning and then before starting work and then again in the evening when we finish.' Amol asked what was the hymn and the girl recited. To his utter amazement he found that it was the *Gayatri mantra*, barely discernible in the Balinese pronunciation. *Gayatri* is a chant of invocation very holy to the Hindu and dates back to the days of the *Vedas*. It is also very beautiful to hear with excellent phonetics and very powerful for calming the mind. But for some unknown reason more than a millennium back the women and lower castes were barred from chanting of *Gayatri* in India. They were also prohibited from the study of the *Vedas* and *Vedanta*. Very orthodox Hindu fundamentalists even today hold on to such views. The days have changed. Now there is no bar but in its place has come apathy, even in learned circles, that it is only history. Hindus debarred the vast majority of their people from the cream of their philosophies and culture and blamed other religions for their downfall. But the powerful idea of an all encompassing formless divinity from which this universe is formed and who is this universe, every portion of which is but a part of the unimaginable whole and who can be worshipped simply in any form one wishes, because every image is but a reflection of the whole, was propagated through the mouths of holy men through ages. Worship was considered a method of Becoming and the entire religion was the method centred on this central theme of God realisation. It was so intense that it has held the society together through the millennia with its multiple apparent variations of worship although very few people understood the intellectual significance of it all. *Gayatri* is an invocation of this formless, conscious, intelligent divinity through the invocation of the sun because the *Upanishad* states that this great intelligent energy of the universe comes to us through the sun and forms our consciousness. Every human being has a little part of this universal consciousness, which is small in quantity but qualitatively the same and can be developed a great deal by effort. How come that these girls in Bali were chanting *Gayatri*? Is it because they got it before the decline of Hinduism in India, which did not touch them because the contact was lost? Amol asked them 'Are you the only people who chant this *mantra*? How about others, how about your parents and grandparents, the children, the workers?' They replied 'everyone does it. The children in schools do it. We have learnt it from our parents and grandparents.' Amol could hardly check himself from embracing them and saying 'Oh, I love all of you so much'. They did not understand what he meant but understood the message of love. They hung on his arms, one or two embraced him from behind as they would their dear ones. How free these girls were! They were admitting about their boyfriends unashamedly which a girl in India could do in antiquity but not for the last millennium until very recent times. Amol said 'Do you know that we have been related for thousands of years?' They said 'Yes, we love you. Do stay with us for a day.' 'How about your work? You have to go when the lunch hour is over.' 'We shall take the afternoon off' they said. Amol regretted 'But I do not have the time. I have to go far to see as much as I can of your beautiful country.' They expressed concern like very near and dear ones that he was driving alone on unknown roads. They implored 'Please drive carefully. The traffic is very bad. Why did you not take a driver?' Amol hugged all of them with his long arms. They said 'Please do not forget us' and they bade him farewell. Amol was transported to another world, another time as he kept on driving. It was a world he read about but never believed. It was still there, here and now. He kept on muttering silently 'I shall never forget, never. How can I? I cannot afford to.'

He drove on and on to the ancient temple at Besakih. On the roadside there were stone tablets, walls with scribbled *mantras* from the *Gita*, the *Ramayana*, the *Upanishads*. There were walled compounds with clusters of small cottages and a central temple that contained no deity. The courtyards were open, unlocked, with no one inside. He entered one and found nobody. As he was looking around a woman came in and stopped at seeing him. But there was no alarm, only a curiosity. Amol gave the usual greeting '*Om, Namah Shivaya*' 'Salutation to Lord Shiva'. The greeting was returned with a smile but no further conversation was possible because of the language barrier. There was only a smile. At last he reached Besakih about a hundred kilometres away on the top of a hill after a steep climb. Here also the worship was to the *Nirakar*, the *Brahman*, the divinity without form. There were small chapels in a large hilltop enclosure in which there were altars, but no deity. There was a notice at the entrance that you should enter only if you want to worship. If you want to appreciate the scenery go around. It did not say that you had to be Hindu to enter, for God is the same to all. People were sitting on the grass under the open sky in groups in front of each altar. They had a piece of yellow cloth around them and had their heads covered. Amol sat in one such group. He was in jeans and shirt with cameras hanging around him. He was sticking out like a sore thumb but nobody objected and nobody took any notice. They were sitting quietly. Were they meditating with their eyes open? There was a priest in front of the group but he was not delivering any sermon, not chanting anything. Like the rest of the group he was also quiet. Then he rose and taking a pitcher poured what looked like water in everybody's palm in turn, which they drank. Another person was following with a plate with some white stuff on it. Eventually the priest came to Amol, an altogether incongruous presence. There was a smile hovering around the corners of his mouth. He poured clear water from the pitcher into his open palm, which Amol drank. He then picked up a few grains of wet rice from the plate and pressed them on his temples. The function was over. The congregation rose, not talking, but silently. Amol did not understand the significance of it all but his mind was filled with a calmness that he could not deny. There were also tall structures in the enclosure that looked like a tall mast sticking out of the roof of a small room with clusters of reed sticking out of the pole like many umbrella at different levels tapering at the top. The whole thing looked like an artificial pine tree. The locals called these structures *meru* but Amol did not understand their significance. He later learnt that these were structures erected in honour of God by the devotees. He later asked the priest at a place called Mengui what did *meru* mean. The priest was surprised 'What? You do not know Sumeru? It comes from you.' Then Amol realized that Sumeru was the mythical mountain, the abode of God and they are creating the symbolism here.

He left Besakih and drove on and on seeing more temples with surrounding clusters of small houses watched by curious inhabitants who did not object. And everywhere he saw the same thing, altars without deities and sometimes not even altars. But the temple or the chapel or the prayer hall was always there in the midst of houses, spotlessly clean. He reached the temple at Mengui. As usual everything was open air with small altars and a small pond, the whole area surrounded by a low wall. Here he met a priest cum caretaker who spoke fluent English. Amol asked 'Where is the deity?' The man pointed to a block of stone in the middle of the courtyard with some etchings on it. Amol asked again 'Which God is this?' The man said 'What do you mean by which God. God is only one.' Amol asked what some etchings visible on the stone meant. The man said 'Those are the marks of the Trinity—Brahma, Vishnu and Maheshwar, or you can say Paramashiva, Sadashiva and Dhyanashiva.' This Amol understood; you can see the Trinity as different entities or as different manifestations of Shiva, another way of emphasising the unity of God powerfully prevalent in India around eighth and ninth centuries AD, especially in central and south India. Actually it is coming from way back in antiquity. The sages in antiquity used only one word to describe all this. The word *OM* has actually three sounds in it like *OUM* denoting the trinity of Creation, Sustenance and Destruction, the three faces of the eternity, the three faces of Divinity. If you went back in time and asked a meditating sage of antiquity what it was all about, he would only pronounce *OM* without spending a lot of words and wasting time. We had forgotten it a long time back until it came back to us, the common men, in the nineteenth century. We are still trying to understand it. But how come these people retained it through the millennia? It was all falling into place in his perception without anybody's teaching. He liked it that way. He also understood why communal harmony was much better in Indonesia than in India. There was very little problem with that until recent times when it is being fomented for political reasons. Were eighth or ninth centuries then the last period of contact with Hindu India? It seemed to be corroborated by the ruins of the Prambanan temple at Jogjakarta. It contained a statue in relief on stone of Goddess Durga with eight hands. That was also most prevalent in India around those times in the south, east and central parts of the country, the seafaring areas. The present image of Durga has ten hands. After this time, for some unknown reasons, the Hindu orthodoxy clamped down on sea voyage. They established the dictum that anybody leaving the shores of India will be an outcaste, a dictum holding right up to the nineteenth century. Another interesting episode occurred at Jogjakarta when he went to visit the Buddhist shrine at Borobudur. His guide was a pleasant, educated and erudite Muslim whose most improbable nickname was Johnny. It was clear from his conversations that he was very devout and very patriotic. While climbing up the Borobudur hills tier after tier he described all the events of Buddha's life depicted on stone. The carvings got reduced as one approached the top until there was none at the top except Buddha statues in meditation inside lotus bud like structures. He explained that it symbolised that as one went higher and higher and approached *Nirvana* all those facts and ornamentations became irrelevant. But at the top they found a boy and a girl engaged in a love game and openly flirting. The guide became very upset and angry at this desecration and started abusing them. This picture became engraved permanently in Amol's mind and the guide became quite surprised to receive a hefty tip at the end of the tour not understanding its reasons. But the guide could not compromise at Prambanan. This was a restored Hindu temple that contained statues of Hindu gods and goddesses that were probably not original but replicas put in by the UNESCO during restoration. In any case there was no worship. But it was difficult for Johnny to go inside as a devout Muslim. Probably he would have had no compunction if it were a *Nirakar* temple as in Besakih. So he asked Amol to go alone and Amol understood and respected it. He thought men were like children. They fought bloody wars over symbols—a cross, the crescent of a new moon, a four, eight or ten armed deity—while the Almighty waited patiently that one day they will grow up. Amol hoped that there was an Almighty or else the symbols will take His place permanently and mankind will land itself in a real mess.

On the last day of his trip, Amol was driving south in Bali, heading for a place called Tanah Lot. It was a seaside resort built around an old temple on the seashore. The temple stood on a rocky outcrop about a hundred yards from the main land separated by a bridge of rocky land that remained submerged in high tide. The temple was accessible only in low tide. The temple was dilapidated and was dedicated to Lord Shiva, as most old things in Bali were. Nevertheless, it was considered a holy place and was also tourist attraction because of nice restaurants in local ambience. Amol got a little late on the way by taking a wrong turn and reached after dark. On the way he crossed a large number of tourist buses and cars returning from the place. When he reached, the very large car parking area was almost empty and the shops were downing their shutters. The restaurants were packed with people, the late dinners. Amol walked down the steps to the edge of water on the land bridge. It was high tide now. The bridge was under water and breakers were coming rushing on the shore. The small temple was silhouetted against the mildly lighted horizon. A medium sized tree was rising apparently through it. It looked very beautiful. Amol asked the only man who could speak only a smattering of English, who came from the bazaar to show him the way, whether it was possible to go to the temple since the water could not be very high on the way. He said it was possible to go but it was risky since the place was infested with snakes and it was their hour now. The man went away. Amol found on his right a lighted concrete terrace. On the seaside end of the terrace there was a high concrete open altar. In the middle of the altar there was a tall pillar in black stone with some etchings on it. A white cloth was loosely wound around the pillar from the top to the bottom and was billowing in the breeze. The whole thing looked like a totem pole. Amol climbed on to the terrace. It was deserted. Another man sauntered in. He was obviously a local in white T-shirt and trousers and wearing a most improbable white golf cap with red borders. He probably had his family with him as two ladies were sitting in the shadows on the parapet on the other side of the terrace.

The man came to him and they greeted each other and started talking. Amol had an instant liking to him. He spoke broken English lacing it with Balinese. Many of its words were Sanskrit or Sanskrit in origin and therefore Amol could understand its general meaning. The conversation actually went surprisingly well. The man enquired whether he was an Indian and a Hindu and beyond that did not ask any other personal question. He was more voluble and forthcoming about himself. He said he was a spiritual person. When asked what that meant, he said that he went wherever people were in distress and when called upon to do so. He would go, spend time with them, talk to them and meditate and generally share their sorrow. Amol asked whether that was his livelihood. He said 'No. I have a small plot of land up in the north about a hundred kilometres from here. I cultivate it for livelihood. But of course people give me presents when I help them and I gratefully accept. Take for example this dress. It was given to me at the place from where I am coming.' He pointed to his very improbable golfing outfit. 'I went to Java and just now landed from boat on my way home. One of the ladies sitting over there is my wife. The other lady has recently lost her husband. So I went to her house in Java. She is still suffering, so I have brought her with us. She will spend a few days with us and then go back when she feels better. There is no money involved in this. God has provided enough for me.' He waved generally around him and folded his hands in deference. Amol felt a little ashamed. He pointed at the old temple silhouetted against the sky 'How old is that?' 'Oh, that is probably eight or nine hundred years old but this one' and he pointed to the stone pillar 'is very recent as you can see.' He said it in such a way that meant that age was not important. Age did not necessarily impart truth or grandeur; the important thing was whether it was living and true. Amol asked what did the pillar mean. He said the same thing as the priest at Mengui. It is the trinity fused into one as different aspects of a unitary God or *Brahman*. 'Why, it all came from you. So you must know. You have really come in search of this, have you not?' Amol was puzzled. Was it really that? Was he searching for something without knowing what it was? His heart was filled with tranquillity and a feeling of purity. He remembered that the people of Bali greeted each other by saying '*Om, Namoh Shivaya*' or '*Swastu Asti*', meaning respectively 'salutation to Lord Shiva' and 'Peace be with you'. These are two immaculate Sanskrit words of greeting from antiquity. Indians have lost them a long time back. The girls of Batubulan and the woman in the courtyard residence had greeted him like that and now this holy man. He also greeted him likewise, being knowledgeable by now. Meanwhile the man was going on talking, not about scriptures or learned discourses, but ordinary everyday conversation about roads, weather, farming and so on. Amol became conscious of his conversation when he said 'Please come with us to our house.' There was real affection and invitation in his voice. Amol brought out a map and asked where his house was. He pointed to an area close to the sleeping volcano. It was about a hundred kilometres away. He had to catch the flight early next morning. He was already a few hours' drive from his hotel. There was no way he could go to the man's house. He told him so. But the man kept on insisting. 'I have a lot to talk to you about, a lot to discuss and a lot to learn. I shall personally escort you wherever you want very early in the morning.' Amol continued to express his inability. He held Amol's hand and said 'You do not understand. This meeting of ours is not accidental, not by chance. It has been preordained and prearranged a long time back that you and I shall meet. We have a lot to talk about.' The man's sincerity was not false. Amol said he genuinely wanted to go, but there was no way. The man was really upset as if the chance of a lifetime was passing him by and kept repeating his request. Amol was surprised but could not fathom it. When the man was sure that Amol could not go, he said 'Well, if you cannot go let us at least pray together in front of Him' and he pointed to the stone pillar. Arm in arm they advanced to the altar on which the formless eternity was placed, two individuals separated by thousands of miles of sea, two brothers separated a thousand or two thousand years back, and the teacher was now the student. Everything else will vanish in this world but the Word will remain as one sage had said. The Word will come back again and again and again, from different areas, from everywhere, in different forms. Amol did not know how to pray or what to pray for. He had never prayed in his life. His only quest was knowledge, not gain or even realisation. He was now faced with something stupendous. What would he say to Him, praise Him, flatter Him, beg of Him? There was nothing to do except to lay his mind bare to Him, naked. Come and reside here. He did not know what the man unknown to him, with whom his arm was laced, was saying. They stayed like that with bowed heads, hands joined in *pranam*. They straightened after some time. The man was holding both his hands and looking at him face-to-face. There was a glow in his eyes, his face serene. He was only saying 'Thank you, thank you' repeatedly. What was he thanking him for? It seemed that he wanted Amol to say something. Amol was silent for most of this encounter, even puzzled. He looked at the man, beyond him at the symbol of fused Trinity of Creation, Sustenance and Destruction, at the roaring dark waters of Pacific Ocean, the silhouette of the temple of Shiva against the sky, an infinity, thousands of miles from his home, thousands of years from his roots and something snapped inside him. He freed his right hand and lifted a clenched fist at the sky and recited in Sanskrit the famous verse from the *Shwetashwatara Upanishad*. 'Hark ye, the sons of the Immortal, I have known Him, the great Being who stands dazzling beyond the darkness; only by knowing Him you can surpass death; there is no other way.' He could actually see the *Rishi* of the *Upanishad* standing at the southern tip of India, where thousands of years later sat Swami Vivekananda in meditation, with his beseeching hands spread towards the seas calling on the people of the world. He did not know whether the man understood what he was saying but his face was glowing. He seemed to understand it all, even know it. He again said 'Thank you' and then went away. They separated and went their different ways without so much as saying goodbye, as if there was no separation. Amol did not know his name, his address, he did not ask Amol's.

The story was so overwhelming that we were silent for quite some time. Then I said 'Was this the spark you were alluding to earlier?' Amol said 'It all adds up to that. Different people get it in different ways but you do not discuss it. It is very precious and you keep it to yourself lest it gets sullied. Because more important than the spark is what you get at the end that is for you to develop. People who have got a taste of this know each other instantly. That is why you do not discuss because you cannot convey it to someone who hasn't got it. It is like Einstein saying "It is very difficult to elucidate this (cosmic religious) feeling to anyone who is entirely without it."

On the Beaches of California

AMOL had gone on a job to Los Angeles. It so happened that this was the time of worship of Goddess Kali at the Hollywood Centre of the Vedanta Society of Ramakrishna Mission. The concept of Kali has exercised the minds of America and in certain academic circles she was a much-maligned goddess. A number of books have been written on her and a number of Internet sites depicting her sometimes even as a barbarian. It amuses Amol to think that Kali must be drawing a lot of academic grants as academic work in many spheres in America is guided by grant worthiness rather than a search for truth and understanding. Some charlatans often work in unknown corners to stay in academia. The Hindus usually do not object because all these superficial so-called observational research do not touch on the core of their religion. It is something like the story of Buddha when he was walking down the road with his disciples and some people standing by the wayside started abusing him and calling him names. Buddha took no notice and kept on walking. Ananda, one of his disciples, was angry and asked him why he did not reply. Buddha said that he did not accept what was being said so the question of replying or opposing was irrelevant. Poincare, the famous French mathematician and philosopher of the nineteenth century, pondered over the nature of fundamental mathematical discoveries, of which he had a fair share. He observed that perceptions obtained apparently irrationally and inadvertently often led to great scientific discoveries. He wrote about these perceptions that 'It is a true aesthetic feeling which all mathematicians know but of which the profane are so ignorant as often to be tempted to smile.' Amol was extremely interested to see whether that aesthetic feeling, which often produced a smile from the profane, existed in the heartland of America.

It was a weekend and therefore convenient. He spent two days in Hollywood. The worship was done with a lot of pomp and devotion. In some respect the devotion was more intense than in some places he had seen in India. There were community singing and community lunches and dinners. The different rituals of worship were carefully done; the fire ritual was done inside a fireplace obeying local laws. There was a huge congregation of people, very few of them of Indian origin. Some of them wore saffron, but obviously only inside the walls as otherwise they would be considered freaks. There was a continuous flow of people, some of them rich and famous, some coming through devotion, others through curiosity. The Indian belief is that it is not important how you go but the important thing is that you went. Sacrificing a weekend in America and going to some other place is interest enough, thought Amol looking at the crowd. At last the two days of worship were over and it was time to bid farewell to the goddess by immersing the image in water. Because of local laws she could not be immersed in a river or lake. She had to be dropped in open sea, the Pacific Ocean, beyond the boundaries of the harbour. This was something novel, thought Amol. On the appointed day the image was taken in a motorcade to a nearby small port. Two large ocean going tugs were hired to accommodate all the devotees. The image was in the front one. There were a number of people with musical instruments singing devotional songs. There were people of all colours, white and brown and black, with all sorts of facial features. It took some time to go up the river and clear the harbour. The waves became stronger and the tug was heaving. The image of Kali was then lifted and gently offered to the ocean. She vanished in seconds. The tugs came back to the port, the devotees disembarked and coming out of the port area, sat scattered on the grassland beside the beach. Small snacks were brought out and they partook of the last communal meal. Everybody was a little sad knowing well that there was no cause for sadness, because the goddess had not been immersed but only her image. But still there was this sadness, as one girl remarked. They then went for a walk along the beach. Amol was walking with a few of the locals. One of them pointed at the ocean and remarked 'This also is infinity.' Amol looked up at the sea and the sky. There were dark clouds in the sky making the ocean appear dark. Dark was the colour of infinity, the same colour as the image of Kali, naked like the sea and the sky. Without thinking he said 'Yes, it seems we immersed the finite in the infinite.' Then he thought more and said 'It seems that the infinite took a finite shape for a small period of time, accepted our worship and went back to the infinity.' He then impulsively took a handful of sand from the beach and said 'Here I have a small portion of the infinity in my hand and I let go and it goes back to the infinity with my prayers. But what I have in my hand is also infinity, in a size that fits my hand.'

Amol went on saying 'Do you realise what happened at that moment? Here I was who never believed in realisation beyond knowledge but in one instant I saw the whole cosmos and myself as a part of it. The finite and infinite are but one, the microcosm and macrocosm are one. I know that in the field of science there is a gulf, a gulf that has to be bridged. But the great indeterminacy that lies in between is really in us. To bridge the gap we have to take care of us. I do not know whether I have been able to convey what I think. I am not that great a scientist. But I knew at that moment.'

I asked 'What is the difference between knowledge and realisation?' He said 'Knowledge is what we acquire, which every student in schools and colleges learn and make use of in pursuing their vocations and profit by it. Only a few go beyond that and realise that what has been taught is not complete. They find the unsolved corners and with that realisation go beyond knowledge and make new discoveries and new knowledge that change mankind. The ecstasy of that cannot be conveyed. People like you and me, ordinary people, can we not get a little bit of that ecstasy that change lives? The concept of Kali was probably there in my knowledge but it did nothing. With realisation it became a part of me, I literally felt it in my bones and started to look differently at a lot of things in the world. I can now describe it in a hundred different ways. Do you see the difference?'

I said 'You experienced it through the concept of Kali?'

Amol said 'Yes, but Kali is not essential to the realisation. It is only one of a myriad ways. Any deity, any symbol of love and respect will do; it can be achieved also through pure reflection. There are many images of infinity all around us. This is what Spinoza advocated—'sub specie aeternitatis'. But Spinoza could not say, as far as I know, how to get there. His was only through reflection and containment of desires. That is a difficult path. There have to be different path for different people. Everybody is not adept or does not like to just reflect. Another way of saying this is that it is all in your own mind. "*Tat Tvam Asi*"—That Thou Art, which is the teaching of *Upanishad*. Buddha wanted people to stop there. Since there is nothing beyond Self, the only way to realisation is the purification of the soul so that it can know the Self. He gave them a simple 'do it yourself' system of ethics to clean their souls. It protected them from the Brahmin priests who, out of greed, had corrupted the original edict of the *Upanishad* and brought it into disrepute. It was a revolution and it worked miracle and gave a sublime religion and culture, which lasted for centuries to this day. But the people could not stay there for long. They needed something to fix their mind to. So deities appeared in Buddhism. Funnily enough the profusion of deities in Hinduism also started at about the same time, in the centuries after the birth of Christ. Very little has been found before that. Buddha left strict instructions not to build his image. But the image was built about four hundred years after his death and the Greeks did it in the Gandhar art. The earliest Buddha statue is wearing Greek sandals and has Grecian features. He also became a deity. Another interesting story is that this profusion of deities of Hinduism and Mahayana Buddhism occurred during and under the Kushan rule of northern India, Afghanistan and Central Asia. The ancestors of Kushan lived somewhere in Central Asia thousands of years back. They then migrated towards China where they were known as Yueh-chi. It was pronounced as Yueh-ti in contemporary Chinese and as Ruzhi in Tokharian, one of the ancient languages of Central Asia. In the second century BC the Hsiung-nu, the ancestors of later Huns or Mongols drove them back towards Central Asia. A small section went towards Tibet. The larger section that came back to Central Asia crept up to Bactria and one principality among them became known as Kushan. They built a powerful empire incorporating North India, Afghanistan and Central Asia and controlled the trade routes. The earlier Kushan emperors paid obeisance to Shiva and later ones to both Shiva and Buddha and deities started coming at that time both in Buddhism and Hinduism. The image of Kali is probably a later fusion of a Buddhist Tantrik goddess with Hindu folklore. The Yueh-chi were a fascinating people. Nothing much is known about them in their first sojourn in Central Asia except that they spoke the Tokharian language. Were they driven out of the place by the great drought that hit the entire region in the second millennium

BC? When they were in Central Asia were they already influenced by the proto-Dravidian culture, which probably extended to Central Asia as evidenced by recent excavations and the presence of the language there in those times? Another people were known to have migrated from the region at the time of the drought and conquered Egypt. They were the Hyksos or "Shepherd Kings" of Egypt and they brought the first word for horse in Egyptian language, which is pretty close to ancient Tamil. How could a people like the Yueh-chi hold on to their identity for so long through such migrations when others were losing their identity? Were they the Indo-Europeans who migrated east while others migrated west from this cauldron of synthesis of civilisation, which was later called Aryan? Incidentally, Aryan, as we now know, refers to a culture rather than a particular people. The Kushans were worshippers of Shiva before they were attracted to Buddhism. Was it the relic of some ancient memory? They were Shiva worshippers before they came to India. Were they so throughout their migrations? Vima Kadphises, the father of Kanishka, was a devotee of Shiva and his coins show Shiva along with the emperor. The empire in his time had not yet made inroad to India. Even the name Vima was from the *Mahabharata*. His son Kanishka, who was the most famous Kushan emperor who ruled in the first century AD, was either a Buddhist or supported Buddhism, but his coins show a pantheon of gods indicating religious tolerance. The answers to these questions are still lost in antiquity but the questions are valid and are based on strong circumstantial evidence. More knowledge of the history of the Kushanas, of Kanishka's grandfather Vima "Taktu", great grandfather Kujula and if possible earlier will throw a great deal of light on the evolution of the modern religions of humanity. All this I am telling you not out of a nationalist urge but to impress that mixing nationalism with religion is really stupid. It is equally silly to condemn image worship without knowing the idea behind it, for all of us, who believe in god, worship one or other of his images, not knowing what god looks like.'

Amol continued after a pause. 'Funnily enough those researchers who have seriously investigated the early life of Jesus Christ and his life after resurrection, point to this area and time. In his early years he is supposed to have gone to Puri and Varanasi to study the *Vedas, Vedanta* and related *Shastras*. He not only read them but also taught them to the low caste who were not allowed that study. The Brahmins and the priests did not like it and they chased him out. He then went north to Ladakh and Tibet and lived for some time at the Hemis monastery in Ladakh where his stay is recorded. Many evidences indicate that he did not die on the cross but went into a trance that was mistaken as death. He was alive when his body was brought down and survived the severe injuries. He then travelled back to Kashmir where he survived and lived to an age of more than hundred years. Peculiar evidences, including DNA studies, indicate that he might have brought back the lost tribes of Israel to Kashmir and it was on his direction that St. Thomas made the journey to India. Even his tomb is supposed to be in Roza Bal at Khanyar near Srinagar. I can give you references for all these things but they produce very strong sentiments and leads to unnecessary strife. Though the evidences are becoming stronger, from the point of view of spiritual life of man the actual historical facts are of minor importance and all sentiments are to be equally honoured for they are all trying to reach the same goal. The similarity of spiritual experiences in the scriptures of all religions is a direct proof of their universality and not of their interdependence because the things they describe cannot be achieved by copying or aping.'

I asked "Do you mean to say that thoughts akin to those in the *Upanishads* did appear outside India or territories outside Indian cultural traditions, even outside the extended Indian influence in the pre-history in Central Asia, even Mesopotamia and pre-Hellenic Greece?"

He thought for some moments and then said "Yes, I think they did. Mind you, they arose in people who did not care about politics and nationalism. So when you talk about them do not bring in those things. The pre-history is also not a clear-cut picture. But with your question the picture of a serene old man with a white flowing beard comes to mind. Of course nobody knows how he actually looked but that is the picture of the man as imagined and portrayed in a later age. Left to himself he would have left no sign in the world that he ever existed. As he renounced the world and was leaving his country a customs official at the border recognized and stopped him and asked this famous man to write down his advice and experiences of life. He agreed and wrote a small booklet and then vanished into oblivion. That book is Tao-Teh-King and the writer is Lao Tse. What he wrote in that booklet is today known as Taoism but he did not write it as a new religion or sect. Professor Suniti Kumar Chattopadhyay writing in the 1950s put Taoism at par with the *Upanishads* in revealing the deepest spiritual perceptions of man. But Lao Tse was probably only one in a line of spiritual thought from ancient China and there is no historical evidence of a communication between India and China in those times. There must have been many such people in this world who are not caught by a customs official to divest their knowledge and they are often not eager to talk or write about things that can only be obtained through the deepest perceptions, introspection and meditation. There are evidences of this in Buddhist scriptures. But it is said that their thought and mental power continue to influence the humanity. I do not know anything more about this. I am only repeating what I have heard or read about, just as a storyteller, which is neither here nor there. Lao Tse was born in 604 B.C. and what the subsequent century gave to the world! It gave Lao Tse and a little later Confucius in China, Buddha in India and Thales of Miletos, the philosopher scientist and father of scientific rationalism in Greece. The highest philosophies in the world had given birth to both spirituality and rationalism and both came from the deepest perceptions of man. Confucius had actually undertaken a journey to meet the aging Lao Tse, a very interesting meeting indeed. One was contemplating on the spiritual rationality of man and the other on political and administrative rationality of the society."

I asked 'How was the edict of the *Upanishads* corrupted?' Amol replied "anybody cannot go and proclaim that 'I am He'. The scriptures definitely wrote down the characteristics of such a man and the stages he has to go through that has been seen in the life of sages of all religions who have reached it. They will naturally be few and far between, those that had attained and not merely on the path from where they can fall due to temptations. But the scriptures were lost to the masses and some of the priests wielded magical powers, which can come without much effort and have to be discarded in order to proceed further. People did not know this and were influenced by magical powers. Devotion took command over reason. They will be influenced by magic even today. Shankaracharya retrieved the texts of the *Upanishad* in the eighth century A.D. and through his short life he engaged in debates with the Buddhist masters or Acharyas to prove the fundamental nature of the *Upanishads* and won. These texts and debates have been carefully preserved but women and low castes were still debarred from its study. The priests and the monks did not give up their preserve. So the knowledge did not disseminate to the masses until the nineteenth century, until the advent of Sri Ramakrishna and mass printing technology. Printing gave access to the common man to read the scriptures and the life and teachings of Sri

Ramakrishna provided the interpretation. He interpreted the scriptures in simple terms for the common man as also the intellectuals and gave them equal right of access to the knowledge. The practical side of his teachings as explained by Swami Vivekananda and those who followed him are for practical applications to society, to create a society of peace and harmony and knowledge, the human society of the future. Shankaracharya established ten lineages for Hindu monks or *sanyasins* and even today most of the *sanyasins* belong to one or other of these ten lineages in their initiation, but can go thereafter as far as his spiritual powers will take him. He belongs to an order but without any material link, unlike Buddhist and Christian convents and orders. Even Sri Ramakrishna along with the entire Mission belongs to one of the ten orders. With Muslim invasion, Buddhism got obliterated in India, Central Asia and many other places, but Hinduism survived."

I asked 'But why should people be so worried about God or whatever it is? In the modern times to most people God is only an embarrassment giving rise to so much strife and tensions and bloodshed.' Amol said 'that is the great mystery of mankind. God exists even today in this technological era. It seems to be a basic inner urge and therefore cannot be ignored. And the same Word comes back again and again in different forms. Swami Vivekananda had said that they come back about every five hundred years. The coming of Buddha, Christ and Mohammed are indeed separated by roughly five hundred years. Reformers, sages and saints followed them for reinterpretation of the Word. But every new coming is somehow translated into a new territoriality. Those who equate religion with territory take over, sinking humanity in further despair. Those who have the real knowledge often stay clear of the disputes. This is what man does to the Word, but somehow it lingers to come back in renewed vigour and contemporary form and the great veil of *Maya* is lifted slightly and for a short time. Those who see they see, others don't. It is said that such cycles are a part of the game of Creation.'

I asked 'How did Buddhism decline?' Amol said 'Oh, there are many reasons. I do not want to go to all that. Basically over the centuries this dynamic and humane religion bred laziness. But then religions also obey the second law of thermodynamics as explained by Ilya Prigogine and you know his work on thermodynamics. They go into organisation and then disorganisation. The best of them connected with man's perceptions survive and go into organisation again. That is happening in Buddhism too. In fact it is happening in every religion and the territoriality is also coming back. This is how the world goes on. We did not order it. Our duty is only to understand. That is essential for the future of the world.'

The Man in the Street

WE had a light supper and sat down with brandy and coffee. We had hardly talked during supper, filled as we were with our own thoughts. Amol lighted a cigar, which he was fond of having after dinner. After he had a few puffs, I asked him 'Is it time to come back to India or should we view the world a little more?' Amol smiled and said 'This whole exercise in roaming all over is to bring you out of your restricted shell and to show that you really existed in the world, in the universe, in infinity. Without that view the truth will not appear. Remember what Spinoza said about viewing yourself in the background of eternity. Up until Kant the western civilisation was trying to become something. After that they only wanted to possess, to build, to conquer. Thank God they did so or else we would not enjoy this brandy and cigar. But when you have to see yourself you have to see in this whole background, not restricted to your back garden. Remember the edict of the *Upanishads* 'This *Atman* will not be gained by those who are not brave and strong.' Please note this double emphatic negation. With that we will come back to India. But it is difficult because we shall have to look deep down.'

There was a chauffeur in Amol's family since his college days and he worked for a long number of years. His name was Mahendra. He had seen Amol grow up and used to call him 'Dada' affectionately. They chatted a lot and Mahendra used to pass on his simple philosophies of life to Amol. One of his favourite philosophies was regarding money and earning. He used to tell Amol many a time 'Dada, remember one thing. Never in life hanker for wealth that is not legally and morally yours. Such wealth does not stay and does not bring happiness.' He was a government employee to start with and continued to work in Amol's family after retirement from his government job. He practiced what he preached and was a scrupulously honest man, a rarity in his profession because most chauffeurs used to steal petrol and spare parts. He had four sons and used to live in a small mezzanine room in an old dilapidated house. Amol had often visited the house. His wife used to live in his village home occasionally visiting the city. He used to go to his village only during planting or harvesting seasons because he was serious in his duties. He had a tiny piece of land that produced some rice but not enough to last the year. But whatever it produced was an extra bonus, at least from his point of view. With his meagre salary he kept his family happy. This was always a surprise to Amol. It represented to him the eternal India; there was no reason why they should be happy. It was not reasonable from a purely economic point of view. He put all the sons through college, every son earning a little by private tuition of junior boys from the time they were in the upper classes in school. One of them became an accountant, the second a teacher and the younger two also became professionals. At last the old man could retire to the village where his wife lived and live peacefully tilling his land, which had grown a little bit in size by this time from his retirement benefit money. He was not dependent on his sons. Once in a while he used to come to the city and during one such visit met Amol who had come home on a visit and was delighted to meet the old man. They spent a long time together and when Mahendra left he sat down making a balance sheet of Mahendra's life. He took in all the facts of his sons, their employment and earnings, the fact that the eldest was married and had a kid providing a grandchild for the old man. He put a value on all of them. When he added it all up it ran into millions. On the side of input there was very little concrete apart from the meagre salary of six hundred rupees a month or about fifty American dollars in contemporary exchange rates. The two sides did not match. So he put a big 'Q' on the input side. This he termed as the idea of a Quality. He got a derived value of 'Q' and it came out to be far greater than any other asset he had. Amol was amused that he had invented a formula for the balance sheet of life. He then made his own balance sheet and was amazed to find that with the value of 'Q' Mahendra was almost at par with him. He then made balance sheet for some of the people he knew and saw to his surprise that Mahendra could match them any day with his big 'Q'. Where the 'Q' was weak it was not compensated by wealth. Mahendra had of course suffered to keep his 'Q' constant. He must have suffered jeers and taunts from his colleagues for being so honest and not earning a little on the sides. Worse still he must have suffered grave doubts about himself, off and on. But he survived, because he had a few thousand years of culture behind him. The slogan that must have egged him on was not 'If you are clever why aren't you rich'; it was 'If you are clever why aren't you honest?' One needs some intelligence to stay honest in today's India. Though not formally educated beyond the primary level Mahendra had that hereditary herd intelligence. That must count for something. The problem is that we do not have one universal 'Q', or yet to find one.

One day Amol was standing at a street corner. An old man in tattered clothes was sitting on the road painting the number plate of a car. He was doing his job patiently and immaculately. A string of cars were waiting to have their number plates painted. For some reason there was a rush. The owners were egging the old man to hurry up. The old man looked up at one of them with quiet dignity and said 'I cannot do any faster than this. A bad job will spoil my reputation.' When a man offered him extra money to jump the queue as other owners had left their cars and not waiting, he refused it with scorn. Amol thought he should be promoted to the position of chief executive of one of the big industries, which were making losses. He wondered what sustained him to be so honest and so full of dignity. He realised that the man must have achieved it by keeping his needs within his means, however meagre those means might be. He remembered the Greek philosopher Diogenes who did not want anything from emperor Alexander. His only request to the emperor was to step aside and not block the sunlight by his presence. It was the control of need that gave a man honesty and dignity. The problem though is that augmentation of need and heightened desire is necessary in today's world to achieve economic development or a communist revolution, whichever way one looks at it. How to define the golden mean and who would do it? But something has to be said for containment of need, looking at the world today. We need to have greed beyond our need to keep the wheels of economy turning. The whole consumer industry is up to its neck in this. But where is the end? Disposable goodies, disposable cars, disposable wives, disposable people, shouldn't there be an end to it somewhere or should the whole world go up in smoke from unfulfilled and unnecessary desires? The terrorist acts round the world, the Osama Bin Ladens of today are made from economic jealousies, from unfulfilled desires and by augmented desires for power and indulgences of our biological lives. They are tagged onto religion or nationalism or something else and the whole issue gets confused. The 'Q' value of Mahendra and the man in the street is a drag on economy, a despair of politicians, but is of high value. How to reconcile these?

I cut in at this stage protesting against this wholesale condemnation of desire. I said 'without desire there will be no progress, no development. It is the desire of man that makes the civilisation progress. You eliminate desire and you eliminate development.' Amol agreed to a point but not entirely and said 'Yes, desire there has to be. In fact it is not possible to conceive a man without desire. But what sort of desire is desirable? Here also man has to place himself on a larger canvas than his own egotistic self. It is Spinoza and Vivekananda all over again. The desire for common good that are unselfish are the instruments for development. You will say that also starts from basically selfish desires. That may be true sometimes but not always. It is not important where it starts but where it ends. That produces development of the society and also the individual. The economic laws and ethics have to undergo a sea change before humanity achieves it. The gluttony of one nation cannot last. A new economics has to come. After all, desire for God is also a desire and even that can go haywire if not controlled and channelled and can produce bizarre psychological effects.' He continued. 'Let us look at it from another angle. Satisfaction of desire brings joy and happiness. We are selfish and possessive about desires of our biological life but there are other desires and joys of aesthetic life where we are not possessive like great music or art or poetry. In fact we derive greater joy by sharing with others who are able to share it. Here, even if for a limited time, we are forgetting our narrow restricted self. Why should man find joy in forgetting his egotistic self? All our desires, beyond the bare necessities of life, are formed in our head and they are limitless. So it is possible that some of us will have desires only or mainly for that joy outside our narrow egotistical self and their number is increasing. You can be there through arts or science or music or through service and spirituality. Whereas the first three need some gift or capability, the last ones are in everyone's reach as a way of finding joy outside the prison walls of our ego. That joy is enormous and its aesthetics is the only thing that can save the individual and the society. It has to percolate in the society, not only metaphysically but also through practical economics. Today's capitalist economy is not suitable for that and it has to change or it will crumble. The economy by today's laws can either go up, in production, profit, share and stock and currency values, in GDP, whatever parameters you apply or it will go down. So there is a continuous tension, a continuous push to increase consumption, a continuous augmentation of desire. But it cannot be available to everybody in the whole world in equal measure. Economic laws have to evolve so that mankind does not remain a continuous slave of desire. New parameters have to be added and a steady state economics has to evolve. The rich societies of today are as much in danger as the poorer societies. That is because the world economy is actually floating in thin air. The danger has always been there after the crash of the thirties. But the threat is more real now because it is coming not from nations but from people cutting across national boundaries. It is coming because the value of labour is so different around the globe. You earn much less than me doing the same or similar work because I work in an affluent country and the value of your money is so little. Among different kinds of labour who is to judge as to what labour is more important to the mankind? An inverse correction is being attempted by adding value to your product to make it less competitive in world market. The rich nations through their various organisations are trying to maintain their economic and political advantages, when what we need is some sort of a global socialism by consensus. Modern methods of production are increasing the leisure of man, at least in affluent countries. Some of this surplus energy and resources have to be diverted to the poorer nations. The joy of sharing has to come in force if the world has to survive and the economics has to be altered accordingly. This sharing has to be through an economic system and not through aid. Humanity has to be considered as a single entity; your brother has to be seen as your own self. Even higher apes are probably capable of feeling some of the unselfish joy as is being shown by recent research. The whole thing is contained in the process of evolution and is continuing in the psycho-social evolution of man. Through the conflicts and turmoil of history man is continuing on that path. If we fail we will be destroyed.'

We were silent for some time. I was immersed in my thoughts and he in his. I was not prepared to give in so easily. I had my doubts. At last I made a comment. "The two human examples you have given have a common flaw. They involve two people who had no possibilities, at least not much of it. It can easily be described as forced contentment, forced by the circumstances. The honesty is laudable but it may be a matter of habit and not deliberate. Can you give an example where it is a deliberate decision and in a person with possibilities who is not a monk? I ask this because similar situations can be found in nationalities who find violence easier than the arduous task of development."

Amol thought for some time and then said "as usual you have a point and I like you for that. You will not accept anything without reason and it is a great help for my rationality. Firstly, all nations have the possibility of development. They have to find or be shown their best route. To answer your comment on individuals one person comes to my mind and I shall tell you his story. I had known him intimately for the last years of his life. He was a professional and quite good at that. In the early years of his life he was involved in revolutionary politics. He went to jail and for some time was put in solitary confinement. He was a smoker and liked his cigarettes very much. But in solitary confinement there was no possibility of having a smoke since such prisoners were not given class one treatment. He used to die for a smoke but one had to beg the jail warders, mostly without success. One day a warder was smoking a cigarette and dropped the burning butt just outside his cell and walked off. He was so desperate for a smoke that he tried to retrieve it through the iron bars of his cell. Suddenly he stopped in the act and, as if from outside, looked at himself. How ridiculous was his behaviour that he would stoop so low just out of a habit of desire when he was being punished for selfless sacrifice for a cause. At that moment he gave up the desire and withdrew his hand. That withdrawal at that very moment lasted him throughout life. He spent his life in service to the poor and the oppressed vowing never to earn from his profession for his own livelihood but use it for others. He even gave up politics in which he could have gone anywhere, could have reached the top, because it would give him desire for power and position. A brilliant organiser he worked everywhere at the bottom rung of the ladder without ever occupying a visible position but he made a change everywhere he went both in the organisation and the people around him. Few people could follow his high examples and there were frictions but he never blamed anybody. He went on working quietly, leaving one place and going on to another without bitterness, but always to the poor and the oppressed. He had married a woman who loved him but made it clear to her that he will never earn. They had a child and the wife worked to maintain the family. He remained unattached, busy in his social work and yet was a loving and attentive father and husband. He gave them the best he had. He had so much dignity that the high and mighty treated him with respect. There were many who loved him but were overawed by him and were unable to follow his ideals. But he was unconcerned even to their failure and remained kind and friendly to them. Long after his death they still come together on his birthday to share his memory. More important than that he was effective and successful in the projects he undertook. I shall not go any further because you will identify the man and he would not have liked that. It is hard to believe that he lived among us in this country. He understood very early in his life the bondage of desire and the freedom and dignity in its absence but he was not a monk, just an ordinary person like you and me. There are such people all over the world, may be not many, but enough to make a difference."

I thought I knew whom he was referring to but refrained from comment. I did not know the man that well. Amol continued "this is of course an extreme example of living without desire and very difficult to follow in the society. But even a little less is extremely good both for the society and the individual. But let me go to the extreme on the subject of living without desire and what it may lead to. That is also good for the human society though it may not be immediately apparent. I shall leave that judgement to you. I shall tell you two more stories. It is such a pleasure talking to you. Who else would have listened to them?"

On The Himalayas

AMOL, during one of his visits, went to see two holy places in India, high up in the Himalayas. They were the temples of Kedarnath and Badrinath. Actually he wanted to visit them from his student days but never had the time. Perhaps he was only now mentally ready for them. He aimed at Kedarnath first. To reach the temple you had to drive to a small base hamlet, spend the night there and then trek for about fourteen kilometres up the mountain to reach the temple at about eleven thousand feet altitude. One can also take a pony or a small carry basket with bearers. The climb is arduous at places and one has to start early in the morning to reach in daylight, as it is difficult to find an accommodation after sundown. Throughout the trek the river Mandakini gurgles down the rapids in its narrow bed in the gorge beside the road. In the ancient texts Mandakini is the river of the heaven. Amol reached in good time going part of the way by pony as the climb had become arduous without acclimatisation. He checked into one of the few guesthouses, which he had booked earlier and went to see the temple. Without knowing it he had arrived on a full moon night. Every full moon in India is auspicious and each one of them has a name. This particular one was called *Gurupurnima* or the full moon in honour of the Guru and on this day every believer in India pays obeisance to his or her *Guru*. The *Guru* may be a spiritual *Guru* or the favourite deity or the *Guru* of dance or music. Amol had no knowledge of this never having had a *Guru*. The temple was a small one standing majestically in a valley surrounded by high snow capped mountains on all sides. On one side of the temple the Mandakini flowed as a narrow stream, its rush reduced by the comparatively gentle fall of the valley. A flat courtyard surrounded the temple and apart from some visitors there were a few *sadhus* or hermits with matted long hair piled high up on their heads. One of them was sitting in one corner of the courtyard surrounded by a group of Europeans. Amol sauntered close to the spot to try to overhear what they were talking about. A young man was showing some photographs to the *sadhu* and they were discussing something. The photographs were not from India. When he came within earshot he was surprised to hear that the language was not English, but some East European language in which the *sadhu* was also conversing. He could only hear some words. By now he was almost indecently close and eavesdropping. The *sadhu* suddenly looked up, saw him and spoke in clear Hindi 'Son will you please bring me an '*atta ka parat*'?' Amol was a little ashamed and moved away saying 'Yes'. He did not have the foggiest notion what was the article the *sadhu* wanted him to buy. He asked around and learnt that it was a sort of perforated metal plate with a high brim that one used to sift and knead the dough of flour. It was available in local shops, which he decided to buy later. But as he moved around in the novelty of the place it went out of his mind. He loitered around the courtyard as darkness fell. There were very few visitors now; they had gone home or to the food shops below. It was rapidly filling up with *sadhus* of varied appearance but all with long matted hair. Some had it hanging down like a ponytail reaching below their knee. In others it was piled high up. They had sparse saffron cotton clothing casually thrown around their body though the night was quite cold. They were minding their own business without any communication to anybody. Some of them were circling the temple continuously, others were singing or just quietly sitting around. Amol was watching the one road that came up to the temple and the surrounding slopes to see where they were coming from but could see nobody arriving. The snow peaks and the hills were glowing in the moonlight with not a cloud in the sky. The Mandakini was glowing like liquid silver and he could trace it almost to the distant silver mountain and the glacier from where she came. There was not a single 'civilian' on the courtyard apart from him and the hordes of *sadhus*. It was quite late in the night. Suddenly a *sadhu* stopped him in his tracks. He had matted hair piled high on his head, his body was smeared with ash and his bright eyes were looking from his ashen face. He was wearing a blanket loosely like a toga. It was clear that he was completely naked under it, as the blanket was too short and flimsy. It was probably only a concession to the gentiles, not much good as protection against cold. The *sadhu* addressed him in a nasal tone in a forced manner as if he was not much used to talking. He said 'Son, I am hungry. Can you give me some food?' Amol said 'Yes sir' and rushed out through the road towards a cluster of shops. It was late and he hoped that at least one shop would be open. He went into the nearest food shop where the shopkeeper was very busy. It was a thatched hut full with people wanting to buy food. The shopkeeper was an one man show, frying *puris* or flour cakes in oil, serving on plates made of leaves, taking money and giving change, all in one continuous motion. It took some time to get his attention and Amol asked him for some food to carry. He asked how much and Amol did not know. He blurted out it is for a *sadhu* and as much as he could manage. The shopkeeper was irritated 'Oh, it is for a *sadhu*? Just drop two and a half rupees over there and leave. Can't you see I am very busy.' Amol was flustered. What did he mean by two and half rupees? How did he know how much the *sadhu* would eat and for whom he was buying? He tried to ask but the shopkeeper was very busy and very irritated. 'Just do as

I tell you' was all he had time to say. So Amol dropped two and half rupees and ran to the courtyard to tell his *sadhu* to go and eat before the shop closed and order more if he so wished. But he was nowhere to be seen. He searched for him everywhere but he was not there. Rather bemused and upset at not being able to explain anything Amol thought it was time to go back to the guesthouse. It was after ten at night. The valley was still glorious. The crowd of *sadhus* had thinned but nobody could be actually seen leaving. It was also bitterly cold. As he was turning for home he remembered the order for '*atta ka parat*'. Amol thought that the *sadhu* must have gone home or wherever they went. It was very late and very cold and he had not seen him since the late afternoon. But on second thought he started for the shops to see whether anyone was still open. They had downed their shutters and it was dark. The oil lamps were no longer lighting the street. If he could find the thing he would buy it and keep it as a souvenir even if the *sadhu* had left. He found one shop where a faint light was coming through the closed shutters. He knocked on the door and after the second knock the hatch was opened a crack. The shopkeeper was having his meal. Amol asked for one '*atta ka parat*', which the shopkeeper kindly gave in exchange for a few rupees. Amol chose a medium sized one, which will be good as a souvenir. Then he started for his abode through darkness. As he approached the corner where the *sadhu* sat in the afternoon, which was on his way, the tall *sadhu* materialised as if out of darkness hovering at least six inches above him and asked 'Have you brought my *atta ka parat* son?' Amol was startled and brought out the plate 'Yes sir'. The *sadhu* took the plate from his hand and vanished in darkness. Amol stood there for some time and then went his way.

Amol was silent and pensive. I asked 'so, what did

you make of your experience?' Amol said 'I do not know.' The whole experience was so eerie. Things happened next day also, things I cannot explain. You know that I am not given to mysticism. I am a hard-boiled materialist and rationalist. But I realised that I should not have an opinion on things I did not know about either way. Many of these *sadhus* are highly educated like this last *sadhu* I have talked about, some of them even brilliant professionals though they will never let you in on this having left that premonastic life. But I happen to know some of them. There was another thing I remembered the next day. It is a verse from *Brhadaranyaka Upanishad* where Rishi Yajnavalkya says "The ancient sages, it is said, did not desire children, 'What shall we achieve through children, we who have attained this Self, this world.' They, it is said, renounced their desire for sons, for wealth and for the worlds, and lived a mendicant's life." I am quoting from a well-known translation that kept the original Sanskrit form. This *Upanishad* probably came in its written form around 700 B.C. Who were the sages ancient even to them? How come that the same line, the same search is continuing for thousands of years? Would it have been possible if it was just hearsay, just lies? I do not have answers to these questions. Millions have trundled this path for thousands of years. My ego is not so high that I would think that all of them were fools and I am the only intelligent one.

After another period of silence, which were becoming longer and longer, I said 'so thereafter you proceeded to Badrinath. Was it a recurrence of the same experience?'

Amol said 'No, it was completely different. I was disgusted the moment I landed. The same crowded, bustling and confused Hindu temple town with bus stands, honking cars, beggars, soliciting priests promising heaven, the middlemen, the shops selling all sorts of ware where the most precious commodity was toilet tissue paper. The loud speakers were blaring out devotional songs, which dried up the last drop of devotion I had. I went to the temple and had to stand in a queue with other pilgrims to see the deity. But a little later I found that by paying a little bit of extra money to the priests one could jump the queue. The next day I thought that enough of gods, today I shall watch only the people. There were all sorts of people there—Hindus from all parts of the country and probably an equal number of Sikhs. At that time of the year they come to one of their holy places about fifty kilometres further down. Actually that place is holy for both Hindus and Sikhs. I asked a group of Sikh pilgrims why they had come to a Hindu temple. They were surprised by the question 'Why, this is the place of Lord Vishnu. How can we go back without paying respects to Him? This is our holy place too.' Organised religion in India is such a complicated affair though they do not differ much in their philosophies. There are holy places common to Hindus and Muslims or to Hindus and Sikhs. And yet they fight.'

Amol sauntered to the temple in the morning. It was cloudy but bright. There was no rain like the day before. Instead of entering the temple he went to the courtyard in front of the temple and sat on the low parapet wall bordering it. Other people were also sitting there. One of them caught his attention. This was a white man and probably European. He had a very aristocratic bearing, which was totally incongruous in that surrounding. He was very fair; almost milk white, with sleek white hair. He was wearing expensive clothes, foreign in origin. The jeans and jacket of a velvety navy blue was expensive quality as was the milk white polo shirt and white sneakers. He was sitting in a straight line with the temple door staring at it intently without moving or even blinking. He was totally oblivious of his surroundings and the surrounding population also seemed oblivious of him. People were coming to the temple and going inside. There were others who were coming out, but none of them ever cast a glance at him as if he did not exist. There were a particularly large number of Sikh pilgrims that day. Amol decided to watch him and sit him out. He waited for half-hour, then another fifteen minutes and then a full hour passed. The man was sitting in the same pose, unmoving, not even blinking. At last his patience run out Amol was thinking of getting up, when the man suddenly rose and without casting a glance in any direction, started climbing the hill beside the temple, went behind it and vanished. Accepting this as one of the unsolved problems of his life, Amol also got up to return back to his hotel. To get out of the temple you had to climb down a flight of stairs, cross a pedestrian bridge over the river and climb up on the other side into the town. The stairs were lined with omnipresent beggars on both sides chanting monotonously for alms, one of the things that disgusted him. Amol picked his way carefully between two lines of beggars. Before he reached the end of the stairs he looked up to see the sky and was happy that it was really clearing up. At that moment a voice spoke just behind him in a very polished English accent 'It is a beautiful morning sir, is it not?' Amol whirled around. There was a beggar standing in the queue on the right side and smiling at him. He had more than usual tattered dirty saffron clothing with a head cover. He had a craggy unshaved sparse beard and a skin so browned by sun that it was impossible to tell his nationality. The eyes were of a deep blue colour and smiling. Amol was puzzled and went towards him with extended hand and said 'Yes, it is a beautiful morning.

Come, let us have breakfast together.' He said in the same accent 'No sir, only twenty paise will do' and kept on smiling. Amol did not know what to do. There was finality in the man's voice. He dropped a twenty paise coin in the man's hand and walked away.

'So, what was your explanation for all this?' I asked. He said 'No explanation. That day I made a promise to myself not to judge anything, at least not from appearances. Who am I to judge? Who has given me the responsibility or power to judge? My legal brief is only to see and feel and think and trust, if I can. There must be a lot of things beyond my logic. Where are such people coming from and why and for what?' I told him 'I must confess I am a bit surprised. I have friends or friends' friends who have gone to all the places you have so far mentioned. After all these are quite common destinations. But I have never heard anybody having such experiences. How do you account for that?' 'To be honest I am also puzzled. It may be that we sift through our experiences and stock only those that fit our emotions. After all we have lived long enough and there are lots of experiences and I am narrating only those that have moved me. But even then such experiences, I think, will move anybody. Why they occur to me I do not know. I shall hate to ascribe them to anything supernatural. I think it is only a question of tuning of the antenna of your mind and a curiosity and respect for humanity as they are and not judging them with your pre-conceived notions. Ultimately we probably see only what we love to see.'

The Epilogue

I asked whether that was the end of his Indian experiences. He said that there could be many stories but they all boiled down to the same or similar experiences that he got round the world. I told him that listening to him I really wanted to write his biography unless he wrote an autobiography himself.

He laughed out loud. 'What do you mean by that? What do you want to write? I am not even a great man that through the biography you will show how all the indications of greatness were there throughout my life, for the children to read. They are the most contrite writings. So do you want to write my curriculum vitae? In our journey through life we have only a few golden moments, only a few leaves in our tree of life turn gold, only a few buds flower. I have shed them for you. What will you do with the rest of the mundane tree?'

I said 'You have had a very successful life. Travelling through so many countries does not just happen or happen in everybody's life. You have done well in your profession, been appreciated and rewarded and probably even honoured, though you will not speak of it yourself. Do they not count anything for you? Are you not proud of your achievements, not feel attached to them?'

Amol said 'I had a job to do and naturally I did it well to the best of my abilities. It could have been better. Everything can be better than they are. I have had my rewards. I could have had higher rewards if I was better. What has pride to do with it? As for attachment, why should I be attached to my work emotionally? Attachment would have cramped my style. I would have been overcautious or over-reactive. No, no, it does not pay to be attached to one's work in that way. Sportsmen know it by instinct and training. If you are playing in the Wimbledon singles final, you need to concentrate your mind, you need to strengthen your resolve to win, you need to consider your strategy, your adversary and your every move. All that you have to do but not get attached not think about the results. You do not think whether you are going to win or lose while you are at it. You leave that to fate or luck or to God, as you wish. Some young players dedicate it to their dad or mum or sweetheart or country. If you do not do that you are gone.'

'Working without desire, either to win or lose, is that what you are saying?'

Amol said 'No, no, it is finer than that. You work always to win. Your aim is to do the job well, which means to win. But at the same time you do not worry about either winning or losing. You are sure to lose if you worry. The problem is that you will worry if you have a lot at stake and get all worked up. You have to control this stake thing. How you do it is your problem. This stake comes out of extraneous desires, which has nothing to do with the task at hand.'

I said 'I have never heard a more simple explanation of the teachings of *Gita*.'

Amol said 'Oh, I do not know about that. *Gita* must be having a lot of other things to say. But in general the most profound truths are also usually the simplest. When you dedicate the results to God, you dedicate it to a divinity, an eternity and when you do that you ultimately place yourself on the background of eternity and you become fearless. It is not easy but you go through stages. The very first stage is not to be cowed down by the enormity of the task ahead before you have even started. That is just plain common sense. Then there are other stages. This is not a call to crusade or *jihad* but how you lead your everyday life with equanimity and perform tasks that may be small or very big. They are the same to all individuals whether he is a cobbler or a statesman. In the case of a statesman he becomes a '*Rajarshi*' or both a king and a sage, something like the philosopher king of Plato who can bring great benefits to society. See how far the idea had spread in time and space? The problem of winning brings in a whole lot of questions about right and wrong and of means and ends. I do not want to go into all that but, speaking very simply, I can say that the right means make the end more enduring and correct and the only way to achieve the right means is to avoid attachment.'

I looked at him for some time and asked 'Do you believe in God?'

Another guffaw of laughter issued from Amol. 'I knew you would ask that. A discussion of this type must inevitably lead to that. Let me tell you that this is the most difficult question, but I shall try to answer it.'

Amol was silent and pensive for some time as if trying out the moves in his mind like a chess player. Then he said 'This is the most difficult question and I would have been very happy to give a simple yes or no as an answer and get away from it. But then either way I would be wrong. For example, I ask you whether you believe that Chinese tea is good for heart and you have never known what Chinese tea is. Anything you answer is going to be irrelevant. Problem is that nobody knows what God is. Everybody has his own idea of God. Some think He is the creator of the universe and some others think He is a father figure who delivers justice. Some think He delivers justice then and there; some think He delivers on the day of judgement and one can have a lot of fun till then; some others believe it will come in the life after. One must define God before he can say he believes or not, like Einstein said he did not believe in a personal God. He had no objection to believing in Spinoza's God. A man like Einstein did not have the ability to define God. But I must define my idea of God for you because I want to answer your question. A man like Einstein can run away and hide in his physics. But I am an ordinary man. I have nowhere to hide. I have to face God, like every other ordinary man in this world. Blessed are the meek for they shall inherit the earth.'

Amol was pensive again, took a few sips of his brandy and started again. 'In all my travels what has struck me most is the innate goodness of man. Now, this is a very hackneyed word. It is found even in Anne Frank's diary and seems like hopeless hope of the weak. But if you analyse it, it has great merit. Man is naturally cruel. He is in fact the cruelest of animals. He kills without reason; he even takes great pleasure in wantonly killing his own species, which is against natural law of self-preservation. He also knows evil, to a degree unimaginable in other species. He is rapidly becoming the master of his own destiny and therefore extremely arrogant. But underlying all this there is an innate goodness in man that you get to see more easily if you travel and interact. Why should it be there? The only reason I can think of is that in spite of these follies and deficiencies compared to other animals, man with his higher perception feels an innate goodness in the universe, in the nature. Since he is a creature of the universe he feels it in his own heart. Please do tell me if you have another explanation. This is why Paris is somehow kept from burning, why a desperate finger somehow does not pull the trigger on the nuclear, biological or chemical missile at the last moment and again sometimes it does, violating that goodness and repents. These are big examples but there are innumerable small examples in everyday life. And there is of course evil for there will be no goodness without evil. But to keep things simpler let us consider only this goodness.'

'So what is this goodness that humanity feels? Is it an intelligent goodness? You may disagree and say that it is a stupid goodness because its causalities are all wrong. But then it is the same thing, two sides of a coin. So whenever man projects a quality on this thing that he feels, it takes on the appearance of two opposites, an automatic duality. Therefore to avoid projecting any subjective emotion or quality of our mind, without which we really cannot think of anything, let us just call it a consciousness. We perceive it as goodness because that is helpful. In reality it may not be directly responsive to the everyday affairs of the humanity. So it is an impersonal goodness. The moment you give it that quality it will bounce back that it could also be personal. But leaving aside the questions of personal or impersonal, it still suffuses the universe and modifies our world-view. This experience of goodness produces some change in you, it cures your narcissism. Remember we discussed about narcissism in our centre of love. The centre of love in us is concerned with more than just choosing the next bed partner. Just remember Dr. Strangelove and the bomb. Getting rid of the narcissism you see this flow of goodness in different levels, in different hues, through all cultures, through all levels of different cultures in different patterns. This gets rid of your intellectual stand aside pluralistic relativism, your supercilious deconstructive post-modernism and raises you to a more universal affinity and kinship. In other words it opens your centre of love to a much larger universality. This is the beginning of spirituality, a rational spirituality. Different people get it in different manner. I am talking of only one mode. Expansion of your centre of love to include the universe gives you a quality that the humanity has always associated with godliness and then you have an integral view of man, with his body, emotions, desires, intelligence, rationality, perception, spirituality and environment, both physical and biological, in every cultural, economic and technological scenario. Humanity has been searching for millennia the ways to such integrated universal personality and the search has become more intense in recent times due to improvement in communication and strains of techno-economic societies. This is good but on the downside it is producing a 'new philosophy' almost every two years. In this raucous marketplace understanding has become as important as knowledge. Ever since the birth of man he is searching for the Reality in one form or another. Why? It is not really because of his failure to explain the natural phenomena. The greatest natural phenomenon is man himself and his inability to explain the incongruities in his life drives him to search. In the process he searches for the causality in the environment around him and his knowledge is increasing, the veil is lifting, but the Reality is continuously receding into the darkness just beyond. It still stands in the shadows between light and darkness. It still is in him.

"Let us take another strategy. Man is continuously trying to lift the veil on Reality and he is using his intelligent conscious mind. His consciousness comes out of what? Is it a new synthesis in the universe? That is highly unlikely without precursors. An assumption that it came out of nothing will be against the logic of science, as we know at present. So there has to be a proto-consciousness in everything that goes on to build consciousness. Or you can call it a protomentality, a term that I think was used by Whitehead and by Abner Shimony in recent times among others. But I like to call it proto-consciousness. It was necessary to make even the first bacteria a few billion years back since it also has an information processing system and is one of the earliest precursors of life and consciousness that survives through reproduction and natural selection. An amoeba has an information processing system that at cellular level is akin to man but not man as a whole. It can 'think' of its immediate environment but not the cosmos. The whole process of evolution can also be seen as an evolution of consciousness, an evolution of brain. Once the brain came into being its development, as seen in the development of its frontal and fronto-parietal regions from the amphibia to the higher mammals, has been almost linear whereas the rest of the body has undergone tremendous metamorphosis forwards and backwards to make it adaptable for survival. Another linear development has been in the development of the heart, from a single chamber to two chambered, three chambered and four chambered heart and the functional benefit has been the supply of greater amount of oxygenated blood to brain accepting a higher probability of heart attack. If the direction of evolution is only towards survival of the species then there are many life forms that are more efficient than man in survival and reproduction. If the increased efficiency of the information processing system that we call intelligence from an amoeba to man is projected further in equal measure we cannot even imagine the outcome. Intelligence is not entirely synonymous with consciousness but it is the most obvious manifestation of consciousness. This consciousness must then be accepted as an integral part of Creation. We literally must be swimming in consciousness, which may be another dimension of energy that our science does not yet understand. Since we are trying to reach this consciousness and find the journey to Reality difficult, is it possible to make a direct contact? Scientists will object. We have to progress by their path only. But the objectivity of science instantly includes two different and opposing qualities. The separation of the object from the subject, which is the basis of scientific logic, is proving a barrier to understanding the structure of Reality because either the process of observation is changing the object or the subject is an integral part of the object. Integration of observership with the objective is yet to come and will probably come in the form of a new mathematics, but not in my lifetime. Just think how entropy is finely balanced in the universe. Gravitation from matter exactly balances the free energy so that the sum total is zero. The universe started at zero and is still at zero. Yet you and I have a concrete existence in it, albeit for a short time, until we go up in smoke or in the dust generating some free heat and some debris which goes on to make may be a rose or an apple or part of a galaxy or a baby's limb in mother's womb or a million bacteria. Yet in this short time we think of the cosmos, find out the physical laws that govern it and leave ourselves to chance. Can you comprehend that? Science is also sometimes based on assumptions. Take for example the Euclidean definition of a point and a line. A point is something that has no length, breadth or depth and a line has no breadth. Can you imagine such an ethereal thing? Yet on it are based our largest cathedrals, mosques and temples. So let us at least examine this other path. Though we are finite, can the little bit of infinity in us, like the handful of sand on the beach, make contact? Plato said it was not possible, you can only get an idea, an idea of good. Plotinus said it was possible. So says the *Advaita Vedanta*, but goes on to say that non-dualism and dualism, between you and this universal consciousness will be closely entangled so that you will view it from a distance till the last. That is why there is no objective proof because when you are in it you lose your discerning individuality. This is what Plato says in his caveman simile. What happens when you make contact? Here I have to depend on hearsay for I have no direct experience. It says that ultimately you go beyond time and space, which means you cease to exist as a separate entity, because our existence is only in reference to a space-time. But in the process you feel and radiate great beauty and harmony and lose the fear of death. You feel it even if you go part of the way. Feeling it in miniscule quantity is what gives man goodness. Before you merge you have a great vision beyond space and time, future and past coalesce, you lose discrimination or it becomes minimal and you see the entire creation as but your own self. The goodness that comes out of you benefits the whole creation. This is what has been said. This is what I can say about God and I find it plausible. I only say it is plausible because

I have not been there and I shall not rest till I reach. Only after I have been there I shall be able to say 'Yes!'

We were silent. I was pensive. It will take a long time to digest what Amol had said. I was startled by his laughter. He was looking at me with an impish smile hovering around his lips. 'I promise to let you know when I get there but I do not know how. I do not know whether I shall be able to say 'Yes'. I can always leave a sign though, like breaking that big branch of the tree over there. But sadly my friend, you shall be put to a lot of trouble explaining it to others.'

I was silent. He looked at me quizzically and patted my hand. 'Oh, do not be so depressed. You can always find some believers, in every walk of life, in every sect. You can find some believers for almost anything. They often pull down the veil as hard as they try to lift it—one of the funny contradictions of life. But what can we do. We have to live with it. That is why we have to keep reason alive but not allow it to become a veil too. Belief in reason is also a belief. They intermingle surreptitiously. One needs to be very alert. It is a difficult task. But it is also easy. Truth is always easy with a little bit of faith.'

His mirth was infectious. I smiled too. I could see a little bit of what he was saying. For the first time in this discourse I started to relax. 'So what do you plan to do when your working days are over?' I asked. 'Will you go to the jungles, like the ancient sages, before you break the tree?'

Amol had an expression of mock horror on his face 'what, go to the jungle, like Britt? What for? I am happy here, shoving and bumping in to people, looking at life and getting a lot of fun. Some sorrows too, but that is all part of the game. No, no, my friend, can't you see that this is the jungle. Here I stay.' He waved his hand around.

I said 'I shall like to meet Britt once to get her side of the story. We are discussing her all the time without giving her a chance. That is unfair.'

Amol was serious now. 'So you shall, my friend, may be so you shall. Life has a habit of throwing up impossible coincidences. I shall also like to meet her once more. I have to straighten out a few things too. That is, if it is possible to straighten out such things.'

After a pause he spoke again. 'I have told you about our last day together but not how we parted. As she came to the door to see me off, she said 'do you remember our car crash? You drove like a maniac at something like hundred and forty kilometres an hour on that slippery road in that small car and we skidded, catapulted to a somersault and then rolled down the hill. The car was completely smashed scattering into bits and pieces all over the slopes and the hulk landed on the trees but we were miraculously saved unhurt. We walked up the hill to the waiting police car. They eventually let you go because you had almost killed us trying to save others on the road. You were so stupid to drive so fast. You were really trying to kill yourself, were you not?' I did not answer. Maybe I was trying to kill myself, kill myself in that space-time capsule, because it would never come back. She was also silent. With her hand on the door handle she looked up 'I was not alone then, I am alone now.' It was only a moment. She composed herself immediately and smiled. I whispered 'You are not alone.' I was lying of course. All of us are lone travellers. We get companions on the way for variable periods of time but we have to complete the journey ourselves. The journey is the ultimate truth in the universe. All of us, the world, the galaxies, the universe, all of us are on a journey. We know not where. The destination is unknown, but we have to move and move and move. That is your only right; there is no other option. 'Charaibeti', I said as the *Rishi* of *Upanishad* had said in antiquity. She knew that too, smiled and kissed me and said *'Trâffas igen, kâra vân.'*

'Charaibeti means you have to continue the journey

but what did she mean?' I asked. 'She said, 'shall meet again, dear friend' he replied and fell silent. He continued after a pause in a low voice as if muttering to himself 'you know I did want to kill myself. But I also switched off the ignition as we were flying through the air before the car hit the ground, I was that cool. Which one was real? Was I trying to go beyond love because it hurt too much? Going where, for what? Was it for a love that did not hurt or was it just self-preservation? How long do I have to search? I do not know. I acted by instinct. That is deeper than intellect. I looked death in the face and sidestepped. What for? To go somewhere beyond love? I wonder.'

* * * * * *

It was late. Amol had to catch his flight next day. I promised to meet him at the airport to see him off. At the airport I found him flustered and arguing with a porter. He was relieved to see me and said that the porter was asking for a lot of money and he had no cash. He thought the porter service was on courtesy of the airline. The taxi had cost much more than predicted. He did not know how the taxi driver managed to cheat. I looked severely at the porter and paid him off. Amol checked in. I was wondering whether he was losing his proverbial ability to handle people when he came back for a final farewell and said 'Thank you very much for last night. It has given me much to think about. Do not think I have said the last words.' He went through the gates. He did not go through the walls; he did not fly on his wings. Suffering the world like any of us he seemed to carry it light, something that I did not have and did not know. The meaning of his name struck me then. Amol meant untainted.

In Search of Perception

I did not hear from Amol for a long time. It was impossible to reach him unless he did. He was always on the move. My letters were either not forwarded to him or he did not reply. Then after a long gap of nearly two years a letter arrived.

Mon ami

I received all your letters asking about my whereabouts, my health and all that. There were also a lot of underlying questions. I did not reply because you are special to me, the keeper of my golden leaves. I cannot reduce you to the mundane level of ordinary news. I had to wait till I had attained some maturity to shed more leaves. It is for you to judge their value. I have been thinking a lot about our evening conversation. What an amazing evening! We sat down for simple chitchats, to exchange information of what has happened in our lives in the meantime, having met after so many years. And see what happened. My deepest secrets came tumbling out along with my feelings and perceptions that I have never expressed to anyone. It was not all my fault; you had an equal role to play. This is what happens when perceptions coincide. In any case it has done me a world of good. The deepest thoughts in my psyche have come out into my conscious mind. Maybe I had thought of one or two things, but they came out in a string with you. Since then I have thought a lot, meditated if you must know. I have been astounded by what was in me. All this must mean a lot of garble to you. So let me try and put it down in an orderly way. You shocked me by asking about God and I gave some very ordinary and superficial answers. But it worked on my insides and churned all my experiences and my life. Out of that churning came insights and awareness of deep recesses of mind that I was not conscious of.

Looking back on my life and my experiences as I catalogued and stored them in my mind I now think that my whole life was probably spent in search of God. I should not use that term because it will mean several jumps at one go that will confuse the issue. It is better to say that I was looking for something permanent and unchangeable inside me that went beyond customs, ethics, religions, successes and failures. Very early in my life I decided that if I did not find such a thing on what do I base myself. If I did not find a gem in me that was equally valuable in an igloo, a tepee, a desert tent as also the high and mighty skyscrapers of wealth and knowledge, then what do I live by. That is what has restlessly driven me round the world to see and share as many lives as I could without being tied down to a particular set. I started off with sex as a light evening chat. But I have really been places, from the high and mighty to the so-called ordinary. And I think I have got a glimpse of God, the unchangeable beyond all the temporal changeability. I say I have only got a glimpse but more correctly only a feeling of its presence as if in a sixth sense. That is not enough, but it is at least a starting point. This is where faith comes in, which is not enough, but important as a starting point because it keeps you going. Lots of people stop here and go no further. But I am an investigator. I have to be there, I have to see God, if He is there, be in Him, face-to-face. I have five thousand years of experience behind me, the experience of the search. But it has never been described or rather described in various ways for it is intimately mingled in all the changing variables of life and nature, in all the opposites. It is so difficult and yet so easy. In every age there are different obstacles to its realisation. In our age it has been an anathema to science until recently. Let us examine it through the objectivity of science and rational philosophies of our times.

Let me first think what is this 'Perception' that I have

mentioned. Let us try and define it. To me it is a suprapersonal rationality of man acting on his object of ideas? Not knowledge acquired through the senses, which is the lowest form of knowledge in Plato's epistemology. It is not merely an idea of goodness. It is that magical moment, that fleeting ethereal flight into realisation and knowledge, which is not acquired through the senses or logic. It corresponds to the highest form of knowledge in Plato's epistemology. Does such a thing exist?

In a roomful of different objects two boys are allowed to enter and stay for a minute. They are then asked to give a list of the objects. The two lists will be different. It is an old Boy Scout's game. Why do their perceptions differ? Because the two boys have two different patterns of perception and those objects, which find, so to say, ready familiar sites in their brains are registered easily. If both of them are now asked to write an essay on the room, their essays will also be substantially different. This is why when the facts are there for all to see only one scientist makes the breakthrough.

Dealing with subject and object and their interrelationship has dominated early Greek and Western philosophy. Ultimately the objective won. Objectivity and logic became the cornerstone of human reasoning and conception of reality. The process started from Aristotle and was then incorporated into Semitic religions. But the incorporation was not easy as it came into conflict with the idea of personal god of Christianity even in those early days. Greece did not embrace Christianity till the famous speech of St. Paul from the Areopagos in Athens. St. Augustine, who started his life as a believer in Neoplatonism, at the beginning of the fifth century A.D. incorporated Plato's ideals into Christianity and Plato's academy in Greece was closed. But the old ideas remained strong in the southern part of Byzantium, Alexandria and Spain. These were also the area where Neoplatonism flourished in the second and third centuries A.D. by the fusion of *Vedanta* with Platonic ideals, which also had its origins in *Vedanta.* Its most prominent leader, Plotinus, is reputed to have received *Advaita* realisation that is referred to as mystical experience in the west. The courts of the Achaemenian emperors of Persia in the fifth and sixth centuries B.C. was the great melting pot of Indian philosophy and the west, influencing people like Socrates and Plato. Later, after Alexander, it was Alexandria that became the melting pot where Neoplatonism originated. Plotinus moved to Rome where Neoplatonism was prominent for some time until its integration with Christianity through St. Augustine and others. But the influence of old culture remained strong in the areas around Alexandria, which came mainly under Islam. Infusion of these ideas into Europe through Northern Italy brought about the Renaissance of Europe. The birth of modern science after Renaissance has come into serious conflict with the idea of personal god and has rejected divinity. It is only now that this total reliance on objectivity for an understanding of reality is being questioned as science delves deeper and deeper into the question of Reality in microcosm and macrocosm.

But the doubt should have entered a long time back. We have discussed the assumptions of Euclidean geometry. These assumptions are useful, utilitarian, but were proved to be not entirely correct in all situations. Just because an assumption is useful does not mean it is true. It is only an act of faith that because it is useful it must be true. Today much of the confidence in science is because it is useful. But the deeper it delves into the Reality of the universe and life, thinner becomes its solid grounds. It may be argued that as science progresses further, all these ambiguities will be resolved just as in the past. But it is becoming obvious that such a solution is not possible without solving the problem of Perception.

In the nineteenth century a Hungarian and a Russian—Bolyai and Lobachevski, shot down Euclid's fifth postulate, that only one parallel to a given line can be drawn through a given point. German mathematician Riemann shot down Euclid's first postulate that only one line can be drawn between two points. Thus a whole structure of non-Euclidean geometry came into being. Many people investigated this crisis in the foundations of mathematics, most notable of whom was Jules Henri Poincare, Professor at the University of Paris in late nineteenth and early twentieth century. Bertrand Russell described him as, "By general agreement, the most eminent scientific man of his generation." The details of his mathematical deductions and solutions are beyond the scope of this letter but of greater interest is how he arrived at them and his analysis of that as embodied in his book 'Foundations of Science'. These solutions appeared to him not when he was intensely thinking about the various diverse facts, which were contradictory and only pointed to a void. In his self-analysis he found that the first solution came to him when he was passing a sleepless night, tossing in bed after drinking black coffee. The second one came when he was going on a geological expedition and forgotten all about mathematics and the truth came to him by simply looking at a sheer cliff face. There are two other similar situations. Then he analysed the solutions on the background of these experiences and decided that they were not merely intuitive. He realised that among the large mass of varied and contradictory objective facts he had actually chosen those that contributed to the greatest harmony of the most. He actually formed the hypothesis that it was his "subliminal self" that made these selections. It was beyond intelligence and beyond intuition. What is the subliminal self? It is self at its lowest intelligent intensity. It is the stage of uncluttered mind when perception becomes acute. Poincare must have endured a lot of smiles in the prevailing atmosphere of nineteenth century Europe with materialism and determinism at their peak. But what about now, when we are at the beginning of the third millennium? I quote from a contemporary, Sir Roger Penrose. He has written, "The arguments from Godel's Theorem serve to illustrate the deeply mysterious nature of our mathematical perceptions. We do not 'calculate', in order to form these perceptions, but something else is profoundly involved – something that would be impossible without the very conscious awareness, that is, after all, what the world of perception is all about." Do you see how selfish and jealous these scientists are? They want to keep perception only for themselves and want us, the common people, to stand aside. Have we no right to this ecstacy?

Another great scientist of our times, Albert Einstein is not so jealous. I quote three lines from his writings. "The cosmic religious feeling is the strongest and noblest motive for scientific research", he writes, and again, "It is very difficult to elucidate this feeling to anyone who is entirely without it." The cosmic religious feeling must be contributive to the subliminal self of Poincare, where the ego is at its lowest. And this feeling of subliminal self is very difficult to convey to someone who is driven by ego. Further on, he writes, "How can cosmic religious feeling be communicated from one person to another, if it can give rise to no definite notion of a God and no theology? In my view, it is the most important function of Art and Science to awaken the feeling and keep it alive in those who are receptive to it." Let us take the last sentence first. Why does the scientist write about art? Is it just because he was an amateur violinist of more than average calibre? Imagine listening to Beethoven's Fifth Symphony or an excellent rendering on the Sitar by Ravishankar. It gives us immense pleasure. Aldous Huxley had written once that listening to the ninth symphony in the dead of the night gave a feeling of God. I do not remember the exact words but it was something like this. Personally I have felt as if the inanimate objects come to life. Why do we get this pleasure? There is no objective material gain. What is this pleasure that is beyond self? We are transported immediately to an immense joy, which is beyond self—Suprapersonal. Similar is the case in literature and the visual arts. Those that can impart this pass the test of time. The objectivity of western philosophy has always been in difficulty in reconciling this with the logic of mathematics and science. Einstein equates this with the ecstasy of science. It is interesting that the things that are hotly contested have already fused together in the consciousness of man. What about us then, the common people, who are not great composers or great scientists, can we not be in this joy? Are we different creatures than the high and the mighty? If it is so, their science and their art will have no meaning for us and it will indeed be a sad day for humanity. In that same sentence Einstein says that it has nothing to do with God and theology. It is important to ask what Einstein means by God, as the word God means different things to different people. Einstein has himself said that he does not believe in a personal God delivering justice and punishment or reward. He believes in Spinoza's God. And what is Spinoza's God? Spinoza denied that God inspired the Bible down to the last letter. He was declared a heretic and deserted by his family. He led a lonely life practising his profession of polishing lenses. He identified Nature with God. He said God is All and All is in God. He said every individual is an expression of something infinitely bigger. Everyone should see himself in the background of this eternity in order to achieve true happiness and contentment. It is our passions—such as lust and ambition, which prevent us from achieving it. Get rid of your lust and ambition and you will see yourself as a part of eternity.

Ah, I can see you my friend, smiling and slapping your knees. You want to say to Einstein 'that's right; so when we get rid of those whatever remains is God. *Tat Tvam Asi*—'That Thou Art'. You are smiling because whatever I have written so far is pure *Vedanta*. It almost seems like a class of practical *Vedanta*. The difference between Spinoza and *Vedanta* is that Spinoza does not say how to become what he asks people to become. It is not easy to control lust and ambition. *Vedanta* shows not only the end but also the way; not just one way but a myriad of ways according to one's individual nature and inclination; each one of us is capable, each one of us have it in us, provided we know the right way. We are all sons of the immortal. It emphasises that whatever remains in the state described by Spinoza is not a remnant but a concrete positive thing that grows, that which is called God. That way *Vedanta* is not just a theology. Each *Upanishad* is a thesis showing a path to the perception of God. But at the same time they say that what is sought to be described is beyond description. Only the path to the realisation can be described and only an idea given as to what lies at the end. The God that Einstein cannot believe in is the Judeo-Christian personal God—the extreme dualism of God, his son Jesus and the human sinners. We have known for a long time, for a few thousand years, that dualism is devotion, where man looks at God as being outside of himself, sometimes with supernatural qualities, with ten arms and so on. But for the seeker on the path of knowledge, God is ultimately *Advaita*, the enlightened Self; when he realises Him he says '*Sohaham*', I Am He, because in me lies all the mysteries of Creation. You can ultimately reach it both through the paths of devotion and knowledge and at the end the two fuse together. The path of knowledge appeals to the objective mind and it is necessary to follow it as far as it would go but objective knowledge by itself cannot reach the end. At some point perception and faith beyond logic becomes necessary as in science as described by Poincare and Penrose. But *Advaita* is an incomprehensible and dangerous philosophy to the general mass of people and can be abused. So definite stages have been set and definite character features described for he who attains this and near the end he has no desires left. This is the same in all religions. Those stages can also be attained through devotion. A devotee can also attain enlightenment at the end of his quest when he perceives unity with his object of love. But a devotee even ultimately likes to keep God at an arm's length in order to keep his devotion. With Christianity this is the only way possible, the path shown by St. Francis of Assisi. Western scientists, from Copernicus to Galileo down to the present time, rebelled against this God of dualism, of an external causality, because it did not correspond to their idea of reality. The Christian church needlessly persecuted them. With extreme dualism akin to a tribal culture they wanted God to be the ultimate external causality of everything. It was not there so much to start with as shown in the gospel of St. John. One would suspect that a lot of factors like property and territory were connected to it. We too have been needlessly drawn into this argument forgetting our own heritage. There is no conflict between *Vedanta* and science. In fact they are complementary to each other and often *Vedanta* sets the questions of perception for science. I have it on authority from Professor John Wheeler of Princeton University and Professor Niels Bohr and incidentally both of them are well versed in *Vedanta* philosophy. Remember the cosmology of the *Brhadaranyaka Upanishad*. In the beginning there was only One. He has been called Viraj, which means Great or just Presence. He woke up and there was fire inside. He thought that I am alone. I cannot even know what I Am. Then he divided himself and with every division He produced an identical but opposite pair until the whole creation came into being. But the initial question remained. Who Am I? I have not put it inside quotation marks because the three thousand years old language is different and so is the social situation and therefore a lot of similes have been used. Mankind had not yet thought of Big Bang. While using ordinary language as opposed to mathematical language we still deal in similes. What image does the word 'subatomic particles' bring to an untrained mind? Does it not bring the image of a handful of pebbles? If human civilisation gets destroyed and its mathematics is lost but the language remains, a future intelligent generation will think that our idea of the universe was that it was made of Ping-Pong balls. A lot of ancient mathematics has been lost. We do not know how our ancestors worked out the positions of stellar constellations before and after their time and embodied them in monuments that have survived. A lot of advanced mental mathematics is contained in a mnemonic form in the *Vedic* literature that is only being understood now.

Most ancient philosophies put man in the centre of the universe. *Vedanta* did not limit consciousness only to man, but ascribed it to every living and even inanimate objects. Man has it in the highest concentration, which is his only pride of place. It is something that we are wondering about today. I have told you about Abner Shimony attributing a protomentality to the particles that constitute the universe as an explanation of the indeterminacy of objective reduction at quantum interface and the structure of human mind and consciousness. Let me give two more quotes from his writing to refresh your memory. 'Potentiality is the instrument whereby the embarrassing bifurcation between dim protomentality and high level consciousness can be bridged.' At another place he writes 'from a Whiteheadian point of view the hypothesis that the actualisation of potentialities is achieved by the psyche of the perceiver is not as ridiculous, anthropocentric, mystical and unscientific as it is commonly regarded to be.' These statements on actualisation of the physical reality and human mind are also valid for actualisation of potentialities from ordinary human consciousness to supramentality. This is what spirituality and approach to divinity are all about. They are neither mystical nor irrational. This approximation of science and spirituality is the great excitement of modern times and it may seem that the quote may well be from the *Upanishads*. Many physicists think that life and consciousness cannot be outside the immutable and fundamental physical laws that govern the universe. The whole phenomenon of biogenesis, the origin of life, is an extreme organisation that has to be paid back in an equal amount of disorganisation to maintain the thermodynamic balance of the universe. How and where does the payback happen? Incidentally, there is a *Tantrik* imagery of Kali that has created a great confusion among intellectuals and they give it a sexist connotation. In this imagery She delivers a child and then gobbles it up by swallowing. Do you see the connection with what I have just said? The great indeterminacy that lies between microcosm and macrocosm both in science and in philosophy is somehow linked with the consciousness of man. Without a resolution of this the whole problem of Being cannot be resolved. The problem that makes Niels Bohr exclaim his famous utterance, "To be? To be? To be? What does it mean to be?" during a discussion with Heisenberg and Hoffding on the Uncertainty Principle. Some people like Penrose think that this will come through a new mathematics. Others like Hawking think that a discussion of consciousness is unnecessary and superfluous to determine the structure of the universe. Some people like Barrow think that this gap is not merely limitations of our mental categories but intrinsic properties of reality and hence an absolute limitation upon any attempt to understand the ultimate nature of the universe. Most people think like Wheeler that since observership is an important prerequisite for the understanding of reality in microcosm, an integration of observership with the observed is essential for an understanding of reality. The subject and the object have to be integrated. Meanwhile objective research finds organic molecules, even amino acids and the possibility of bacterial spores in the interstellar space, in the comets and its signature in other planets like Mars. Was earth seeded with life by comets, from Mars, from space? Still the question remains, how did they originate first and where and why? Scientists can create amino acids from elements in the laboratory under specific conditions. They can even produce RNA, but these are not the same as those producing life or degenerate when they are made to replicate. Only the left-sided amino acids are concerned with life. Why? In nature and in laboratories both the left-sided and right-sided forms occur in equal proportions. A solution of only left sided forms gradually change to a mixture of both forms. But life chooses only left-sided ones. Because they are made by enzymes that are specific for left-sided ones and these, in turn, are so because the DNA that make them are also specific. It is possible that the cause and effect are *vice versa*. It is hard to believe that so much selectivity can be the outcome of random chance and non-purposive. You will laugh if I say God make them do it. But probably you will not laugh if I said that the force of consciousness in the universe, which we are yet to discover, has its own method of functioning and actualising.

I hope I have been able to confuse you badly. So now I shall come to the biologists. They agree on the role of the electron in life's processes including the functioning of the human brain. They have seen the microtubules in the structure of cells from the unicellular organisms to the neuronal cells of the human brain and the passage of energy through them. These are somehow connected to the functioning of the brain but just how, is not understood. Here a large-scale quantum condensation may be involved.

Let us look at the origin of life, biogenesis, from the

biologists' point of view. Unlike physicists they cannot accept integration of biogenesis with creation of universe and consciousness. Because, they say, it will then give biogenesis a purposiveness, which is not guaranteed in Darwinism. It may, in addition, provide a back alley for the unwanted return of a divinity. They will prefer to call biogenesis a chance, an accident, occurring in some primordial soup and then a deterministic Darwinian process of natural selection to take over. Darwin himself was never drawn into speculation on biogenesis saying that there was not enough data. Can you accept that, when we do not ascribe the birth or death of a star to chance, the birth of a galaxy to chance, we have to ascribe the birth of life to chance? We, who find out all these, have to leave ourselves to chance. Can you understand why Darwinism will be undermined by integration of life with universe? The laws of physics work beautifully in the macrocosm in spite of the indeterminacy that lies underneath. Why should Darwinism be undermined by integration of life with universe, making life inevitable in the universe? There is a simple solution. Let us describe divinity as intrinsic and not extrinsic. This is described in more than one *Upanishad* with a beautiful simile. The seawater is salty wherever you taste it, anywhere from the North Pole to the South Pole. But the salinity differs according to the concentration of salt. It is highest when solid salt is formed. A doll is made from solid salt and life is breathed into it. If it then wants to fathom the ocean from where it came, it will be dissolved in the attempt. Divinity is everywhere but is concentrated at certain points. Its highest concentration or organisation so far is in man. Will it reach a higher concentration in some other form in the future? Julian Huxley wrote in the last century that such conjecture is unnecessary as man himself is evolving. He had written 'Purely biological progress, in fact, has come to an end, but human progress is just beginning', and he termed this as the 'psychosocial evolution of man'. Darwinian evolution can proceed from the state of dissolved salt to solid salt or from one form to another of the solid state, without any intervention of divinity, just as the universe obeys the physical laws. We have discussed the linear evolution of the brain and the heart. Within any of the branches of the tree of evolution the development of brain has not undergone any significant change. The reptile brain is essentially the same from the early reptile to the huge dinosaurs. There is no qualitative change except in the size in keeping with the body. The development of the forebrain has been the culmination of evolution. In the evolution of other areas of the body such as the limbs there have been a lot of journeys back and forth. For example, a number of dinosaurs, like the Tyrannosaurus were bipeds but that did not lead to a great development of their brain. It cannot be said that freeing of the hands has led to the development of brain in man, as some evolutionists believed. Let us accept the theory of natural selection. But the question still remains natural selection for what. There have been many species that have been more efficient than man in survival and procreation, but have vanished or are staying dormant as living fossils, whereas man can now control even evolution. Can you object if I say that the natural selection has always been for the evolution of consciousness?

You may have started wondering why I have gone into so much science. This is to show that all knowledge is perceptive and increase in the powers of perception is important to man and essential for survival. From the discovery of the wheel to the crushing of an atom the journey is inexorable. Man could have stayed on horseback or even on his feet. The dinosaurs have survived for millions of years in almost the same fashion. Why not man? Because with his greater perception of past and future he suffers from greater insecurity, appreciating and foreseeing danger, and tries to prevent or avert it. This means perception wise the whole of mankind has already risen partially above time. Dinosaurs had no idea that a meteorite could finish them and even mankind did not know until recently, but we know now and knowledge is strength. Man will progressively move to greater knowledge and perception and his physiognomy will also probably change. The move during the last century has been rapid enough to be appreciable. He also has to have a reason for survival. Otherwise all this science will land him in chaos. He has to reconcile himself with his knowledge. Growth of perception and the ability to rise above time and obtain a peek into the future occurs only in a few men throughout ages. After all everyone does not become a Jules Verne or Victor Hugo or Albert Einstein. The rest of mankind just follows suit. With a higher power of perception of the humanity as a whole, man will naturally be able to see further into the past and the future.

But apart from this evidence of perception, say like science fiction, there are perceptions, which bear no resemblance to contemporary knowledge or experience. There are many such examples in our *Puranas*. I shall give only one. In the last part of the *Mahabharata*, both Arjuna and Ashwatthama fired their ultimate weapons in anger and the burning arrows went up with a great roar into the sky, ready to fall to the earth. The gods were alarmed that creation would be destroyed and asked both of them to control their weapons. Arjuna controlled his weapon but Ashwatthama said that he had no control over his weapon. So the gods joined force and diverted it. A situation like this did indeed occur in the sixties during the Cuban crisis. America had the capability to destroy its ICBM in flight but Russia with its polar ICBM carrying MIRV and multiple nuclear warheads did not have the capability to destroy them in flight. The story of *Mahabharata* could not have any bearing with contemporary experience nor with any in the following millennia. 'Arrows once shot do not come back' is a proverb in every language including ours from ancient times. Two of Swami Vivekananda's written remarks may be mentioned to give examples from recent times. He wrote that the ancient Sumerian civilisation was an extension of the contemporary Indian civilisation long before the discovery of remnants of Indian teakwood in the ruins of the ancient Sumerian port city of Ur. In 1895 he wrote to Sister Christine that the working class would rise in Russia and then in China. He wrote the same thing to Hem Chandra Ghosh. He used the word *shudra* in place of working class but they mean the same. Even Marx thought that the communist revolution could only occur in industrialized countries like Britain and Germany, and the Bolshevik Party was not even in existence then. There are many such recorded and unrecorded examples, which are usually not vivid in their entirety and you cannot use them to alter the natural course of events nor do you wish to because a different level of causality has been revealed to you. I cannot entirely discount the story of Alexander and the sage in the Indus valley who reportedly induced him to return. After all, his greatest gift to human civilisation has been the creation of Alexandria, more so than all his conquests. Is it possible to train the mind to greater perception? We normally use only a small portion of our brain in our daily life, just as we use only one lung and less than one kidney. People can train their organs and muscles to become super athletes. Everybody cannot become an Olympic champion but everybody can go some distance to becoming a champion. Similarly it is possible to exercise the brain and increase its power of perception. Voluntary control of the autonomic nervous system is well known, as is conscious withdrawal from the sensory world, not to feel pain. There are many people who have seen or heard such things. But even such will-power, power of the conscious mind, faith, and conviction are not ends in themselves, but only means to an end. You have probably heard of Neurotheology, a new subject that studies the brain in spiritual experiences and searches it to define God. The study has been stimulated by the similarity of such experiences across cultures and religions. At least that much has been recognised by science. In experimental neurotheology the experiences like the sense of dissolution of the self or similar experiences are being tested. Some interesting observations have been made and people wonder whether our brain has made the God or He has made the brain. Collectively they are called mystic experiences and can be obtained through other means such as music or by autosuggestion or self-hypnosis. In the path of spiritual attainment these are called initial experiences that are easily attained and have to be ignored and eliminated. Only after one has crossed this tempting domain can one rise to a higher rationality beyond mystic sensations. You can tell a man who has attained this by his selfless life and actions and not his words and he actually looks quite ordinary. Perception can then be increased to go beyond time and space. What happens then I do not know, but I imagine a beauty and harmony beyond imagination as fear vanishes when one goes beyond conventional ideas of causality. It would seem quite plausible for Valmiki to write the life story of Rama in *Ramayana* even before he is born because time itself collapses. It is possible that one sees the Einstein-Podolsky-Rosen paradox of non-locality of space-time in operation as solid experiences with human senses. Plato had called this stage unattainable. But *Vedanta* says it is attainable and so did the Neoplatonists—it is an act of faith to pursue it. It is a personal choice whether or not to pursue it—a neo-existentialist choice. But one has to give up a lot in its pursuit—restrain the power of the senses, give up lust, ambition and ego—as Spinoza has said. One has to make the mind uncluttered so that the subliminal self can take over. The pursuit of theoretical physics or of any fundamental science also needs a lot of sacrifice. It is much easier to make an invention and earn money, name and fame. One does not know when one starts whether he will reach anywhere in theoretical physics. That is why in the matter of perception our scriptures say '*nayamatma balahinena labhyah*'—this *Atman* or Self cannot be attained by those who are not strong. Lots of people fall by the wayside—on all ways to perception. But there is a great deal of beauty even on the way. As Rabindra Nath Tagore had written 'My joy is in walking the path'. There is a great deal of beauty in physics—those who trundle the road do it for joy and beauty. One cannot criticise the other's act of faith.

My dear friend, I have been lucky to get only a glimpse of that beauty. Once you have seen it you cannot help but pursue. You do not want anything from this God, no reward or punishment, no power or wealth or happiness. The differences of sex, race, religions, ethics, customs etc. fall away from your mind as you see the unitary nature of the Creation and yourself as a part of the whole. You just want to be there—that what is already within you—your handful of sand. You can call it by a hundred or a thousand different names, but it is all the same. The immensity of this joy, the rapture, cannot be described. I have only glimpsed it from a distance, tasted only a little. Like Newton I can say that I have collected only a few pebbles by the seashore. But it has already filled my heart. I am an ordinary man. If I can feel it, so can everybody. I had told you that I found the idea plausible. I now know that it is possible. I must move towards certainty and open its door. I do not mind even if I die in the process.

I shall let you know when I make further progress in this project.

Yours etc.

Amol

This letter was followed by a long gap—more than two years. Then one day a message arrived by e-mail. It was from an unknown address. It was from Amol.

The Final Passage

Dear ___

I am sending this message from a small mining town on the roof of the world, high up in the north inside the Arctic Circle. I had an assignment here, which is now over. I have finally decided to hang up my gloves. My working days are over. I have lost my wife sometime back. She was a good woman and I was very fond of her. Ours was a relation of companionship and sharing. I miss her presence as a sort of shadow that never interfered but was always there. She did not share my philosophical flights but looked at them with an indulgent smile. Once when I tried to tell her something she smiled and said 'I know you and that is enough for me'. She knew exactly how much to hold and how much to let go, the right mixture of affection and fighting. She will never be taken for granted but never go far. In our last years I tried to woo her back to our initial years. I must tell you that trying to seduce your own wife is one of the finest feelings in married life and a pretty difficult thing too. Try it sometime. It is better that she has passed away before me. She would have found it more difficult than me. She has now set me free. You will be surprised to know that we had actually discussed it sometimes. She did not know about Britt but always suspected that there was someone, in the way in which women know. She also teased me about it sometimes. Our two children have been brought up nicely almost entirely through her efforts. They are nice, with a world-view of their own as they have moved around with us, but firmly rooted in a tradition. They have grown up and now must follow their own lives. I am physically and mentally fit. I am now pursuing a different kind of knowledge and I am very near and you know what it is.

I am at peace as never before in my life. I feel at

complete peace and harmony with the world around me. I feel immersed inside me with an acutely heightened consciousness and look at the world and feel such an intense love as if everything is a part of me. It is difficult to convey this love and joy. The world is very real but is out there a little distance away and its complex causalities appear transparent and you have no emotions about it except a feeling of oneness. The conflict of opposites, the clash of qualities and ideas and emotions, of matter and energy and galaxies and stars, is the drive engine of creation. Without them there will be no creation, no universe, no life, no consciousness and with creation there has to be destruction. But basically they are all the same, two faces of the same thing revealing as a duality. This is the *Maya*, the Illusion, Kali, the mother goddess of creation and destruction. You fuse the opposites and you arrive at *Advaita*, the unitary pure consciousness. You arrive beyond judgment. One day I was meditating and thinking about a beautiful place at the top of a high mountain in the Himalayas where I have once been and which appeared to be God's abode. Suddenly the mountain rose very high and the top went to the very limit of my vision. Like a bird I was flying up the mountain side and I could see all the details in its body. There was dense jungle with tiger and wild beasts roaming in it. There were also many people in various activities. Some were climbing up the hill to reach the top, some had been killed by tigers or died from snakebite, and some had given up the effort and settled down, some had fallen down the steep slope. Those that had given up the climb were either lazing around or had opened small shops and businesses to cater to the climbers or had built big houses and enjoying the comfort and scenery. As a bird I could see that all of them were real but suffering from the illusion that they have reached, whereas the top of the mountain was far above. As a bird if I started worrying about them and tried to take care of them I would get stuck and never reach the top, which is more beautiful than any place on the slope and I can see it far above. Having reached it I may help a few stragglers near the top but not now. I can only feel deep compassion and kindness for all of them. They are really my images. If I now break a wing and fall down I shall be with them. Are you following my story? That body of the mountain with the varied pictures of life embedded in it is the body of *Maya*, the Mother Goddess of Creative Energy and Illusion. Unless you climb it you do not get to the top and you need a guide and help and kindness of the mountain and you have to know how to take it, as every climber of Everest knows.

Having done away with emotional attachment to duality and conflict of opposites you find it difficult to function within its ambit. But fortunately it is never complete, at least not as long as you have to take care of your physical body and its needs. A very rare few can survive in the twilight zone. Others renounce everything, even their own body. I have not gone that far yet but I do find everyday life very mundane and pointless.

There is however one thing I have to do. The thought and effort of that is probably still keeping me alive and kicking. I have to find Britt. I have little less than two months of daylight in this arctic region to find her. I can almost hear your hiccup as you read this. What, after all that! Do you remember that one day in the beginnings of our lives you had asked me whether I wanted to be a monk? I had answered 'that is a valid alternative.' Do you remember that? Of course you do. You have a very sharp memory. At one time I did want to become a monk. Monkhood attracted me because of its infinite freedom and peace. But a monk dedicated to whom, for what? Having studied a little bit of the *Upanishads* by myself I had a vague idea of a formless unitary divinity but did not know how to embrace it and there was no one to teach me. In any case my intellect revolted at the idea of a *Guru*. As I grew up I realised that I can never become a monk since I could not take the vow of celibacy. My sexual desires were too strong. Other desires did not matter. I tried to suppress it for some time and found that it grew even stronger. I gave up suppressing myself. This is when I went abroad and met Britt and our attachment was immediate. In my first sexual experience I found that formless divinity hovering morosely in front of me just beyond Britt's head. I called out to Him and said 'you who are supposed to encompass everything in creation cannot take this little thing? It is also your creation. You shall leave me because of this? In that case I have no need for you. You can go.' He receded but was always there in the twilight of my mind. Sometimes I would talk to Him arguing this and that but He remained where He was. I took Britt as a sex object. Tenderness developed gradually and a great deal of attachment. But still deep down I considered it a sexual experience. The distrust of my own sexuality that has denied me a monk's life and freedom was somehow subconsciously transferred to Britt. I had sometimes considered a permanent bond and marriage but ridiculed myself 'you are one of those fools who marry the first girl that you go to bed with.' Can you see what a rogue I was, but probably the world saw me as a pragmatic as thousands of young men behave that way. Sometimes one's own self is more important than the whole world. Britt was not aware of all this but with her feminine sensibility probably sensed a resistance, a thorn in our relationship. Then came the night, when I gave her that lecture on the innate divinity of man. I brought down book after book on philosophy and literature and read passages to show the moments of exhilaration when one dwelt with one's own self in complete harmony where man actually lived. I did not know half the things I was talking about and I wonder even today. I was feeling a deep tenderness but I do not know how sincere or correct I was. But it hit her. Can you explain that? You tell me that I have the Indian tradition of spirituality in me. What about Britt, did she have such tradition of mentality or knowledge? I cannot blame you because I also thought that she belonged to a different culture. I was not tuned to the idea of universality of man. I knew it but knowledge and realisation are not the same. I thought these were nice words found only in books. I did not know that these feelings are beyond education, religion and culture. They are fundamental to the human mind. She heard it in love and sorrow and she had the feeling without even knowing what she had. I also did not understand until much later. In the meantime our lives flowed in different directions and decades passed. I wallowed in sex for some time to forget Britt and then got married, had children and settled down. All perfect in the eyes of the world. But there was something wrong deep down something was burning. Britt never got settled in social terms. Instead she went off into wilderness. Why? Was it to find that freedom and peace that has eluded me? Or may be she was pursuing that feeling without even knowing what it was. It took me decades to understand all this. Not until that formless divinity claimed me back and, would you believe it, claimed me back through sex. That is another story and I shall not have time to tell you about it. In the process He acquired a form. Form is important. Without form it is impossible to relate to so abstract an idea. And with form comes love. With love comes the ability to understand the pain of others and to understand the world. Only love opens the gates of mind. With love I could understand the pain of Britt. I have hurt her very badly. Has she found freedom and peace in solitude? Solitude does not necessarily bring freedom though it helps. For many years I had doubts about her, whether she is the same as her image in my mind. It is this effort at judgment that has distorted me as much as it has distorted her. She is thus carrying an important imprint of my identity, the identity that probably influenced her but failed to accept her as she was and failed to accept the loving image of divinity. What was that identity that influenced her if it did? She was not a girl given to wanderlust, she was not a girl given to moaning and crying. Then why did she go? I must join her and find out. I have to beg her forgiveness. She is standing in my way as the final illusive obstruction. I cannot run away from it. I must clear it. And then I shall be free.

Oh, how can I show you that my heart is bursting with love, for every living and non-living thing in this world. Everything seems shimmering in gold and everything seems the same. The world is so beautiful; creation is so beautiful. I have never been so acutely aware of it. And the great drama of life is played on this stage. It is like a cosmic dance, the cosmic dance of Shiva. My heart is full, full, full and acutely aware of the world. How can I express the joy and ecstasy of that? I do not remain in it all the time. Some time must be claimed by the chores of the world. But most of my free time passes in it. I must find Britt quickly. I shall search along the shores of the Gulf of Bothania, around the frozen lakes, along the shores of the Baltic Sea. Those are the beautiful places today to get lost. Himalayas are getting crowded. I must find her and I know I will. I had found her once before. That funny story I have remembered only now. It is curious how old stories suddenly come back like old pictures. This was during my first revisit to Britt. The one I had told you earlier was in fact my second revisit.

Before I tell you the story let me guess what you are thinking. You think that I am hallucinating and that I have gone soft in the head having grown old and having lost my wife. That is why I am leaving my job and finding solace in illusion. I am leaving my job because I have nothing more to give. At last the wave of knowledge is passing me by, as it does to everybody. I am no longer at its crest. I can still hang on, I can still teach. But teaching, in my idea, can only be by leading, not by example, not by goading. I cannot fall prey to a temptation, which I have rejected and rebelled against all my life. I have never followed an example in my life, how can I ask others? Let them undertake their own journey and find out for themselves. I do not want to stunt them at birth. This is just practical, not a lack of respect. I am not disgusted with the world nor am I unduly attached to it. My needs have become very small. Many a time, things happen in our lives without our wishing it or wanting it and they crystallise our life and give it a new direction, just as a pattern suddenly emerges when crystals form in a liquid. I could say for better or for worse but I do not know their difference any more. (Do you remember the salt-water analogy of the *Upanishads*?) None of us, from the greatest idiot to the greatest intellectual have ever been able to find rationality in the things that happen to our lives though we always try to explain them through our reason. Some of us go to faith, some of us ascribe it to random chance some of us find laws to govern this. But the laws always fall just a little too short. I can assure you that my rationality is intact, as it always has been and always will be. It has been shown through objective research that sorrow can open new areas of cerebral function just as love can, can make new connections. It may be that I have been able to see faith through reason and I have been able to see reason through faith, and in the process I have gone beyond them both. I know you will ask what that means. It is difficult to answer. It may be that I have suddenly seen a pattern in the crystallisation of life. I am yet to find with what sort of diffraction to understand it, with what agent. A curious analogy comes to mind. You know that DNA can be made into crystals and by X-ray diffraction studies of the crystalline form its structure was elucidated. But if it crystallised inside your body even God will not be able to help you. You will die. They are two forms of the same thing and yet quite different. Chemically they are the same but one in your body is alive while the crystal is not. Nevertheless, if you understand one you understand the other, like life and divinity. Moreover if you put a DNA crystal inside a cell it will probably replicate, that is come to life. So what is life? It is not just the chemistry. It is possible that the chemical reaction releases a force, a form of energy like heat or electricity. That is the energy of life and consciousness. If that is so then that energy must be one of the forces of nature. It must be dissipated throughout the universe. In that case you should be able to integrate it with the other forces of the universe like electromagnetism, heat, gravitation in order to understand the ultimate reality. But our knowledge of this force is no greater than what Luigi Galvani knew about electricity. We are just about seeing the frog twitch. It is a far cry from the nuclear power stations. It may not be possible even to reach that far in the understanding of this life force through science. Because here we are ourselves carrying that energy, which has concentrated into intelligence and consciousness within us and we are using that instrument to understand the world. All our knowledge is getting stored and analyzed by that instrument. With what would you then analyze the analyzer? This is the great question that has been put forward in *Brhadaranyaka Upanishad*, "through what, O Maitreyi, should one know the Knower?" In that same section Sage Yagnavalkya tells his dear wife Maitreyi "my dear, this great, endless, infinite Reality is but Pure intelligence." I want to get a taste of this pure intelligence, touch it if I can. *Upanishad* says it is difficult but possible. Through science if ever it is reached it will not be the science of today. Then again it is not enough just to know. One has to taste it, be in it, and touch it with one's own consciousness. For that to happen my intellect will have to become pure and then this microcosm will be the same as that macrocosm. Then I can touch. Have I been able to convince you that my rationality is intact, in fact never more acute than now?

Since I have brought in Yagnavalkya let me tell you his story. You of course know about him. But his life has a relevance to what I am trying to say and I shall focus from that point of view. Yagnavalkya was a sage in ancient times. How ancient one does not know. Some scholars have put a date from one of his writings that it was written not earlier than seventh century B.C. But it is difficult to pinpoint such things. In any case he was a very learned and erudite man whose writings not only covered philosophy and 'Knowledge of *Brahman*' or '*Brahmavidya*' but a lot more. His social and economic treatise is still followed in some measure in the modern day India. A large number of students from all parts of the known world studied under him. Apart from philosophy, they used to study mathematics, astronomy and all the applied sciences of *Atharvaveda*. Following the customs of those days they lived with their master sharing the household chores and got free food, lodging and education. So Yagnavalkya had a large establishment. He had two wives—Katyayani and Maitreyi and a son from his first wife with the name of Katyayan. Yagnavalkya was very fond of his young wife Maitreyi, who was very learned and took part in the educational curricula. Katyayani's responsibility was mainly to keep the household going. This large *ashram* was provided by Yagnavalkya's earnings from conducting worships and oblations and by taking part in debates on philosophy and logic at kings' courts. He used to beat all the assembled learned men on the subject of the ultimate nature of Reality by his erudition and took home laurels and gifts, which were usually prize milk cows, sometimes with their horns bound in gold. Another woman fell in love with him before he married Maitreyi and wanted to marry him. But her father, who was himself a *rishi*, declined to give her in marriage to a man who already had a wife and a son. Her name was Gargi who became a very learned sage in her own right and used to call Yagnavalkya to duel in debates. She admired him and when defeated asked others not to indulge in debate with this man who was beyond them all in knowledge and perception. Don't we see such women around us even today? Yagnavalkya's debates and instructions in the *Upanishads* were mainly on the knowledge of *Brahman*, the unitary divinity that pervaded the universe and how to attain it. On the state when the immortal self in us unites with that Supreme Self he tells Emperor Janaka thus—"That is his form—beyond desires, free from evils and fearless. As a man, fully embraced by his beloved wife, does not know anything at all, either external or internal, so does this infinite being (self), fully embraced by the Supreme Self, not know anything at all, either external or internal. That is his form—in which all objects of desire have been attained and are but the self, and which is free from desire and devoid of grief." Emperor Janaka is a king and emperor with all the lavish wealth and pleasures of a king, and yet a sage, and so is Yagnavalkya, a sage who has attained all the fame and wealth for his high intellect. How much he must have loved Maitreyi! Tell me yourself, a man of the world, how many times in your life have you felt your external world of senses and internal worlds of intellect vanish in the embrace of a woman? Such a pragmatic man as Yagnavalkya decides to renounce the world, renounce his family, his *ashram* and his wealth. Go out of everything he has built through a lifetime of work. Go where? Go out for that he has known and talked about all his life. But knowing is not the same thing as Being. He goes in search of that. There is a similar story in the known time, only about five hundred years old. Sri Caitanya also defeated the entire learned community of Nabadwip and Varanasi in arguments on philosophy and logic and then renounced his family and his learning to go in search of his Krishna, to Be that which he has preached, a movement that is still continuing. That is another story. But Yagnavalkya does not leave without announcing and goes to Maitreyi before departing and asks her as to which part of his property she would desire. The composer of the first laws of inheritance in India, nay the world, wants to divide his property fairly. Maitreyi refuses property but wants immortality. He then instructs her and this is one of the finest chapters of the *Upanishads* from which I have already quoted. This chapter is repeated again towards later part of the book. The second repetition is exactly the same as the first except the last line, which is, "So you have got the instruction, Maitreyi. This much indeed is the means of immortality, my dear. Saying this Yagnavalkya left." He condensed his entire lifetime of knowledge and gave it to her beloved wife who was also a partner in his quest. Yagnavalkya with his great erudition and learning leaves on an act of faith. This total renunciation has been repeated a thousand years later by Buddha and two thousand years later by Sri Caitanya. In the later ages it was realized that such total renunciation is not absolutely necessary for all men and women except at the last stage if you are able to reach that. The renunciation is automatic along the way as you progress through the stages, like dresses falling off, and total at the end. Nothing is forced, even if you should continue to live in the society for the benefit of mankind. We have had the good fortune to learn it through a great sage of modern times. I shall come to him eventually.

You see now why Yagnavalkya is so close to my heart. However I have not left my wife. You cannot achieve anything by making someone you love unhappy. But I have a pain in my heart. The pain has become dull and distant. Nevertheless, it is there. I have to get rid of it or else my mind will not become neutral. As I sit writing this long letter that will be scanned and sent to you by e-mail after I am gone, an eerie sensation overtakes me. All around me is a desolate arctic landscape where just about two hours of dusk is all that goes for night. Soon the great darkness will descend. Yagnavalkya also departs for the snowy wilderness of the Himalayas. The way my message reaches you would have been considered mythical a thousand or a few hundred years back. So much of mythology is today's practical reality! What man imagines he becomes, he creates. That imagination, that image, seeded from brain to brain over centuries and millennia become reality. Everything you see around yourself has all been imagined by a few. In some cases those images go back thousands of years. Have we ever created anything that was not in our dreams? Maybe it is true that the whole creation is the imagination of a divinity. I want to see him face-to-face. I want to go from Plato's world of ideas to Yagnavalkya's world of Being. It is an act of faith backed by reasoning and a little bit of experience. That ultimate journey is an automatic renunciation. Whether I can come back depends not on me but it is possible.

So now let me tell you the story. I love to tell stories. At least that you can ascribe to my garrulous old age. Otherwise why should I bother to tell you all this? It was Christmas time and I was walking down an icy road with snow falling heavily, in the place where I was. Suddenly I started missing Britt very badly. Just around the corner were the offices of a travel agent. I walked in and asked for an air connection. They said a flight was leaving in four hours, which had a connecting flight to the place and a seat was available. I booked it, went to my rooms, packed a bag and took the flight. I arrived to find that Britt was not there. Nobody knew where she had gone. I thought about it and decided that she must have gone home to her parents. I vaguely remembered that her home was somewhere further north but how to find it? I thought about all the things I knew about her and the people who knew her. Then I remembered that I knew her birthday. There must be some record somewhere. After searching a few government offices I was directed to the church records. It was the last working day before the holidays. I went to the church records and found out her home address. It was a village in the middle of nowhere. I searched for the telephone number but was told there was no telephone connection. The girl at the counter was sympathetic, tried a little more and came up with the number of a neighbour. I rang the number. It was responded. Communication was difficult with my foreign accent. Finally I could make myself understood. Britt was not home but if I could call back in the evening she will be home. I called back. Britt was astounded. She was not expecting my voice. She was upset. 'Why didn't you let me know that you are coming?' I said 'There was no time. But you must come down at once'. She said 'It is impossible. I cannot leave papa now. In any case we live in the middle of nowhere and almost snowbound. We do not have a car and it is miles away from any airport or railways.' I said 'Never mind, I shall get you down somehow. You just be ready' and hung up. While talking to her I had already planned. I went to a friend in the police department. I described everything to him and asked for his help in executing my plan. He literally gaped at me, but the funny side dawned on him and he started laughing. By that time I was already famous in the town, so it was quite in character. The world loves a lover. He called the local police station in Britt's place and asked them to send a cruiser to so and so address and bring so and so and put her on a plane. There was a serious emergency down here. The next day Britt arrived all wrapped up in woollens like a teddy bear. She hung round my neck and called me dumb and mad and stupid. She said 'Do you know, the whole village knows that I have committed a serious crime and been arrested by the police, and that also in the Christmas week. I had a very difficult time assuring papa that there was nothing wrong and I shall be back in a few days. You mad man' and another round of invectives followed, naturally with a lot of kisses. We spent three wonderful days. Then I went away and Britt went back to her parents to spend the rest of the holidays.

You see now that I can always find her? The news of her final journey to solitude also came to me in a similar fashion. We have this thread hanging between us that we can make contact if we really wanted to, whether in the impetuosity of youth or the sobriety of old age. I had approached God with the same impetuosity, challenging him in fact and got caught and, unwittingly, for a short time Britt was a partner, an accomplice. I challenged Him with sex, which is probably the simplest. In everything else I was nonchalant. He took me back in love. So many people defy him with so much. He waits patiently for them to come back. He showed me through a lifetime of search that there was nothing without him and nothing outside him. That he was the loftiest and the lowliest. That he was the high and mighty and also the things you love, like the little rose bush by your door. It is up to him to show you that, up to him to bring you close. There is no high or low for him, his blessings rain down equally, it is up to you to realise and be fulfilled. You leave it to him and he will guide you through the realisations as he is guiding me now to the roots of my life. Believe me it is true. I can replace every 'he' with 'I', but that comes much later. It is too early for that or else I shall again lose my way as I lost it once. I must still cling to the form I love till the job is done. Let me try and explain this to you if I can.

As I have already told you at the beginning of my life the divinity appeared to me as a non-dual formless divinity of monism. This was natural because of my dedication to the world of science and reason. Normally I should not care at all about a divinity. But it was science itself that gave me the idea of a possible divinity and my upbringing might have had a role to play. Like many people in my generation Heisenberg and the Uncertainty Principle might have been the starting point. In any case I could not accept consciousness as a disjointed phenomenon in the universe nor deride it as a purely conscious cerebral phenomenon. But science abhors the personal god of dualism. The mental discipline needed to achieve perception of the unitary divinity is only available through complete renunciation and non-attachment to the world. I thought this was my road to freedom where both objective knowledge of science and reason and the perception of the unitary divinity will fuse in me. Rationally it was all right but emotionally it was not right for me. My heart was not where my head dictated it to be and in this the heart is stronger than the head. I loved the emotions of joy and love and pleasure and my path to freedom had to be within this world, not in the world of renunciation. Above all I had a great hankering for love, to love and to be loved. That is my culture or '*dharma*', which is a much better word, and I am born into it. My freedom has to be in relation to my '*dharma*'. This I did not understand and considered myself a failure. After suffering through life, by the grace of He who is this world and who is in this world, a form came to me. If any credit ascribes to me as an individual it is the honesty of my search through everything consciously and sub-consciously. The whole glorious world of dualism opened up before me, of sight and sound and love and joy. It is glorious compared to the dry asceticism of non-dualism. It is a love that does not bind you but sets you free. Human love creates bondages but divine love sets you free. This is a place where you can live in complete freedom without renouncing anything excepting your ego. You have to sacrifice your 'I' and 'mine'. But you need somebody to sacrifice it to. There comes your personal god. You sacrifice them to Allah or Jesus or Krishna. Then you live as a free man. Think about it. This path is also not easy but tolerable and very very beautiful. It becomes easy once you are in it. Then it becomes just natural. The problem of dualism is of course that it can make you very bigoted. It can make you a very jealous and over zealous fundamentalist. That is why you must remember that there is actually no difference between non-dualism and dualism or pluralism. It is just your culture, your '*dharma*' that makes it so. Divinity is always ultimately unitary and rational with everything, every quality ultimately a part of it. You are approaching it in a dualistic form because you cannot become neutral to all your emotions. Therefore the unitary divinity takes that shape for you, collapses into a particular form, like quantum collapse, because of your mind playing on it. You realise the same thing, rise to the same level as the renouncer and ultimately realise the unitary nature of divinity and may develop the power to switch from one to the other. That is a very pleasant living indeed. You live with a love and joy that does not bind you but gives complete freedom. Dualism has opened this great glory of God to me and I rejoice in it. Things I have never believed in, like visual experience or physical experience of divine form happens though I cannot explain it. But it is concrete and it is real as any other person or object. Why it happens I do not know unless the objective world is itself a reflection of the mind. But I do not want to speak about it because it is not important. You feel the presence of divinity as a concrete thing even if you do not see. How you rise above causality and how time collapses inside you as you rise above space and time is also something I cannot explain. In any case this cannot be a continuous experience and is not the aim. The aim is freedom and peace and absolute calming of the mind and that is the concrete palpable experience. These spiritual experiences that are mistakenly clubbed under the heading of mysticism have been known through our scriptures since ancient times. But they had been disjointed and isolated with confusion of centuries entering the texts through the millennia. One man in our times has searched them as an investigator following every lead and every path and observing both objectively and subjectively at every step and has declared that the core experience that has been seen and described by many people in many religions through aeons of time are all true. He is Sri Ramakrishna and as a man of science I could not deny him. Through his experiences and revelations he declared that you do not have to be a monk, you do not have to renounce from the beginning of your life to be there. The monks are essential to preserve the purity of the knowledge, as people will only trust them in this matter. But even an ordinary person like me passing through life with its usual crazy mixture of love, hate, passions, deceptions and desires can get a taste of that, irrespective of the race, religion and culture I belong to, if only I can sacrifice my ego, forget my 'I' and 'mine' and tune in to the eternal flow of consciousness that flows through this creation, that is tune in to God and know Him to be the ultimate doer even when engaged in our earthly life and work. He never left his wife but took her as a spiritual partner while leading a monk's life. Never before has this happened in the history of religions though it is mentioned in the scriptures. This is a revolution in thought that will influence the world history for centuries to come. Great advances in knowledge have made man's mind receptive and increased his perceptions. Progressively larger numbers of people are able to conceive things that they never thought of before. A great age of truth, the '*Satyajug*' is dawning when more and more people will understand the truth of their existence and the truth about the world around. The fragmented truths in different flows of human activity and emotions will come together and coalesce. Such a message was but natural and necessary at this juncture of human history. The eternal flow of consciousness is neutral to the mundane things that occur in the life forms it creates but at the same time it does react. That which is one is also in many. It only wants its own replication, replication of its own eternal mind. If I can reach it I can get a taste of eternity and see myself in it. My body will decay but 'I' shall get on to something that goes on and on, I shall get to know that 'I'. It is something that goes beyond time. I thereby go beyond death, lose all fear and become calm and immortal. I have that potentiality, it is in me, and I am truly '*Amritasya Putrah*', Son of the Immortal. See how it all comes in? It is really Spinoza all over again. Only this time the path is clearly laid through all religions, all cultures and all philosophies. Whatever you worship in whatever form, in whatever you love, you are only relating to something outside your ego. Push that side of your mind up and up progressively eliminating your ego and you will reach that universal level of consciousness and will be able to see your real 'I' and then live or die in peace, it does not matter to you either way because you have gone beyond your impermanent body. I am only trying to follow that path, without pride and without rancour knowing that I am not the only traveller, not even a special traveller. I am only one among many through the ages through different routes because this is the ultimate aim of life itself. This is the *Upanishad* of Ramakrishna revealing itself at the beginning of the third millennium of our present civilization. The *Upanishads* are really thesis on the path to *Advaita* or non-duality written thousands of years back over an unknown period of time. It has been restated in the modern days of explosion of knowledge showing its eternal relevance. All *Upanishads* have stated that the nature of the ultimate experience cannot be described. But there is a lot of harmony and peace to be experienced on the way and it percolates down to the society. They have also stated that the ultimate state cannot be reached by pure reasoning. Knowledge and reason help in the initial stages, in fact are essential to firm up faith and keep to the right path avoiding magic but cannot penetrate the ultimate because we are part of it and our process of reasoning derives from it.

Even in our image worship, that is the ritual worship of

form, this intermingling of dualism and non-dualism, of God inside and God outside, is emphasised. The ritual is that the worshipper meditates on the divinity within, prays, brings him out and passes into the image to bring it to life. He then treats the image as the living God, as a very loved and honoured guest offering him reception and drink and food and clothes and bed and other facilities to the best of his abilities. He behaves as if the king or the queen has come to his house. He invites friends and neighbours and relatives to meet him and make a great party. When it is time for the image to go he meditates and prays and invites the divinity to come back inside him and stay there. What is outside comes back inside and he requests the image to return again as a very beloved person helping him to realisation. The image then becomes lifeless and is sacrificed in the river or the ocean or the pond. Through the Sanskrit chanting that very few of us understand, this is what is said—very ordinary statements of endearment. Through each practice of worship of the image the worshipper comes closer to the worshipped. Everyone approaches the ideal depending on his intellect and mode of appreciation. Ultimately you are worshipping that which is already inside you.

This is why when the Islam came and kept on breaking temples and beheading images, they could not eradicate Hinduism because the God does not reside in the temples and images but in the heart of every human being whether Hindu or not. Hinduism is after all not a religion but a quest for the spiritual experience and to understand the world. Inside it there are religions and there are philosophies. As an organised religion Islam did not understand it though the spiritual sects inside Islam understood. They did not succeed in eliminating Hinduism in a thousand years nor did the others but they still keep on trying. They did not succeed in the Hindu parts of India, Nepal and Bali where this *Advaita* feeling was high. This is why religious wars and quarrels are absolutely stupid because the divinity is within every human being only the forms vary, from the subatomic particles to the temples, mosques and cathedrals. Many Hindus also do not understand the meaning of their rituals. In my case that image of divinity within has a sorry face, the sadness of Britt, because I discriminated and judged a person. Who am I to judge? I distorted the very foundations of love. It is our ego that makes us desire and also makes us reject. Britt is carrying an imprint of my ego. That has to be corrected or else I cannot unite with Him. I must find her, *Inshallah*. What a beautiful word this *Inshallah* is, gives you such a push and determination and I use it very often. Then when faith rises through your deeds dedicated to the will of Allah you pray and you say *Amen* or you say *Buddhang Sharanang Gachchhami* or you worship your favourite image. Ultimately you realise that what is outside is also what is inside and you say *Sohaham*, there is only One, only One; 'I Am That' and so is everything in the Creation. The macrocosm of infinite consciousness is the same as the microcosm of consciousness in you and you rise and relate to that. Then you are in absolute peace, harmony, and love and beyond desire and your third eye opens. Great compassion rises in you and all judgments vanish. You realise that through all the twists and turns and turbulence of history man's perceptions are rising towards where you are. That is the outside face, the objective social face that is visible and that brings in great changes in your environment. What happens inside only you know, nobody else does. A few close people may see an occasional spark of the unexpected. They may write volumes about it that reveals very little but increases faith and conviction. You stare in awe and wonder at the Creation that such complete, all encompassing and all pervading beauty, grace and love has been given to the humanity and we tear it into pieces and quarrel like wild dogs with the torn pieces. We cannot do much about that because it is in the nature of the Creation but we can make small tiny changes in our short lives and it all adds up and, above all, we can understand. That is the responsibility given to us and to rejoice in that knowledge.

Oh, how can I express what I feel! I know what I am writing seems like gibberish, handed down to mankind since antiquity. I can do no better. I know this is not enough but how can I describe something that is indescribable. For the first time in my life language is failing me. But, oh, how glorious are the impetuosity of youth, the instrument of progress, the excitement of knowledge, which are his greatest gifts, as long as they did not hurt anybody. But I did hurt Britt. Have I fulfilled her in any way? Would marriage have done that or have I given her something more than marriage? If I had influenced her what was it in me that influenced her? I want to see it face to face to know who I was and who I am through this distance of time. I am old now. Our lives came together across a great distance and then they grew in their own different directions. But they got tangled in the roots and an error has occurred there, an error that has affected my life and clouded my perception and intelligence. The veil has lifted. It has to be corrected now. A long time back a covenant was drawn, a covenant of love, it has to be fulfilled now. Or else I shall not be free. I have to find Britt and take her with me. I am not sure that is possible for we are all lone travellers. But I have to try and extend my hand. There lies my redemption. Then I shall be free. Free at last!!!

Adieu my friend.

Amol

* * * * * * *

Years have gone by since this message and nothing more has come. I have not been able to trace him and his family has also failed. The Government has record of his entry but no record of exit. They have also failed to trace Britt. I sit in the stillness of night looking at the tree he pointed to and think about him. Will its branch break? Did he get what he wanted? I do not know what it is. I do not have his intellect or energy and strength to pursue. I have only planted a rosebush by my front door, tend it lovingly and think about him and what he said as I keep looking at it.